Wayward Secret

The Wayward Saints, MC
Book Seven

K. Renee

K. RENEE

Wayward Secret

CONTENTS

DEDICATION

To anyone who has been afraid of showing the ones you love who you truly are. Be yourself, embrace yourself flaws and all.

K. RENEE

COPYRIGHT

Wayward Secret

K. Renee – 2017

k.renee.author@gmail.com

Cover Design: KLa Boutique

Formatting: K. Renee

Cover: © Kruse Images & Photography: Models & Boudoir

https://www.facebook.com/KIPmodelsandboudoir/?fref=ts

Cover Model: Sam Wiles

https://www.facebook.com/SamWiles89/

Editor: Ashley Blevins @ TBC Editing

https://www.facebook.com/TCBEditing/?fref=ts

ISBN-13: 978-1539157915

ISBN-10: 1539157911

PROLOGUE

Elijah

Growing up, I've always known that I was different than my brothers. They always wanted to play cops and robbers, while I'd rather spend time baking with my mom. Of course, they would make fun of me, I hated being the different one, but every day I sucked it up and played the same things they did.

As we grew up, they were always talking about how they were going to grow big and strong and join the MC just like our father, I wanted to be like that too. He was my role model, and sure I wanted to be like him. Hell, I wish I was like him. Maybe then I wouldn't have this secret. This secret has taken over my entire life; it has eaten away at my livelihood for years.

Being in an MC is hard enough, but keeping this secret is fucking torture. I'm afraid to tell both my brothers by blood and my brothers by the brotherhood. They are all so set in their ways, they will probably avoid me as if I were the plague if they knew.

Being the youngest son of the Vice President of the Wayward Saints had its pluses, but it also made me feel like I was alone. No one knew the secret I had been keeping since I was a teenager, I wasn't sure if I'd ever tell them. I wanted to tell them, but they wouldn't understand. I barely fucking understand half the time.

I want so bad to be like my brothers; it kills me inside knowing that I can't. I tried to fuck girls all throughout high school to keep the suspicion off of me, but I was never able to get off. Instead, I always got them off, and then pretended to get mine too When I got older and graduated high school, I finally had more freedom.

Well, I take that back. After high school, I started prospecting at the Wayward Saints. My father and brothers pushed me into it. I had limited freedom. My life revolved around being a Wayward Saint's brother's bitch for the first year. After that, I actually had the freedom I was dying for. I was able to get away whenever I wanted.

I love the Saints and everything they stand for. They are the extended family that I grew up around, they have your back no matter what. Club whores were always everywhere, anytime one of my family members or the Davoli's came around, those bitches were on you like white on rice. I hated their attention, but when I would turn away from them, my brothers would give me a hard time.

I hated knowing that I was different from them. I never fucked the club whores. Instead, I would get on my bike and ride out until I hit a small town outside of Las Vegas.

As soon as the bright lights of the city disappeared behind me, I felt free.

I didn't have to worry about what my brothers would say or how disappointed my father would be if I never found myself an ole' lady. Brantley and Jase both had fucking families now, hell, so did Dominic and even my cousin Gunner was about to be a dad. Everyone was growing up around me, and there were still so many things I kept hidden.

Looking across the bed at where Spencer is sleeping, I remember the first time we met. Spencer is full of useless facts that no one should know, oddly enough I find that attractive. He is the total opposite of me. I'm a biker, and he's in a special crimes unit, two opposite fucking people, one chance meeting and one hell of a ride so far.

The day we met I knew that he was the one. He was everything that I am not, he pushed me to be a better man. He loved me for all of my flaws and never complained when I told him I couldn't tell my family about us.

I could tell it killed him to know that we were never going to be out in the open. Shit, it killed me too. I loved him, I would do anything for him. He was the first person to see me for who I really was and not judge me. Sure my brothers would probably say that they still loved me anyways, but I know that they would judge me. They would judge my lifestyle and my relationship; I couldn't subject Spencer to that. He didn't deserve it.

The longer we keep our secret, the guiltier I feel. Spencer deserves to have someone who loved him as freely as he loved me. That night everything blew up in my face, it was too late to finally say these three words to him. He lied to me. I lied to him. Our secrets almost destroyed us.

CHAPTER ONE

Elijah

Walking into one of the clubs I frequent, outside of the city, I scope the place out and make my way to the bar. This place isn't something that any of my brothers would be caught dead in. For one, there are no women here unless you count the drag queens that tend the bar from time to time. Two, they would probably blow a damn gasket just knowing that I came here.

It's the only place I feel like I can be myself, or the version of myself that I don't show my family. They think of me as the younger brother of Brant and Jase or the son of Nick, the VP of the Wayward Saints. Not one of them thinks of me as being gay. Half of the time, I have a hard enough time with it myself. I feel like I lose more of myself every day that I don't tell them, but I fear for their reactions.

Walking to the bar, I order a beer and lean against the bar with my back to it. Scanning the room, I notice a man standing there talking with someone else. He is nothing like the majority of the men that come here. He oozes masculinity and control. Most of the men that I find here are only about getting my dick in their asses and fucked roughly, not that I'm complaining. I love being able to take my frustrations out on their bodies.

His eyes meet mine for a minute, I can feel my dick tighten against my zipper. My eyes roam over his body, I can see the way his dark jeans fit his powerful thighs and tight ass. The bartender puts the beer on the counter and leans close to my ear and whispers, "He's a sight isn't he?" I turn my attention to her and grin.

"Yeah." I hand her a twenty and tell her to keep the change.

"Thank you sweetness," she purrs into my ear. Turning my attention back to the man across the room, I scan his body and notice the way his shirt fits his arms. He's in shape, but not overly done. I can see a tattoo peeking up through his tee shirt, and part of me wants to get a better look at it. Taking a long pull off of the beer in my hand, I turn my attention away from the delicious man and scan the room again.

Nothing catches my eye this time, and it doesn't surprise me. I typically only come here when I need a release. My brothers told me I needed to get laid last night after I nearly bit one of their heads off for touching my bike. I don't even know why I flipped out on them. Fuck, I don't even know what my deal is lately.

I've watched them all slowly start to fall in love, and it's been fucking hell. Ever since I can remember, I wanted to have what my parents have. I wanted a once in a lifetime love that would take the shitty-ness that we deal with on a daily basis and make it fuckin' worth the fight.

My phone beeps, I see my brother Seb's name on the screen. He and I are probably the closest out of the Insico boys. Brant and Jase were always in their own little world together, and my parents pushed it off on them being twins, which left Seb and me to spend a lot of time together over the years. He's probably my best friend other than River.

River is fucking beautiful and has had a crush on my brother Seb for longer than I can remember. She's five foot five with dark hair that most women would die for. She's everything that I would want in a woman if I was attracted to them. She's funny, smart and the total opposite of us. The good girl with a big heart. She's loyal to a fault, I still don't get why she puts up with me half the time.

Sebastian: Let's get fucked up!

I shake my head at his message and close out of it. If I write him back and tell him no, he's going to ask what I'm doing; I don't really feel like dealing with his questions right now. Before I can look up from my phone, I feel someone brush up against me. A hand slowly runs up my arm, and when I look up, I see the man from across the room.

Our eyes lock again, I can feel his dark eyes zero in on me.

"Hey," he says with a grin.

His hand runs up and down my arm again; I take a step closer to him. He turns to order a drink and then his attention is back on me.

"Hey," My eyes run down his body again now that he's closer, I want to reach out and touch him. The bartender puts his drink down, and I reach into my pocket. Grabbing another twenty, I hand it to her. She takes the money quickly, and I see her smirk.

"I'm Spencer. I don't think I've had the pleasure of seeing you here before," he says. He puts his lips to the glass of whiskey and takes a sip. "I would have remembered you."

Fuck, I would have remembered him if I saw him before too.

"I come every once in a while," I murmur. Men start coming to the bar around us, and I'm forced to move even closer to Spencer. We are practically chest to chest, there is nowhere I'd rather be right now.

My hand goes to his hip, and his eyes practically undress me. Before I can say anything else, I feel my phone vibrate against my dick. Groaning, I reach into my pocket and pull it out. Looking at the screen, I see River's name. She's going to have to wait until later.

"Boyfriend?" he asks huskily. I shake my head no and pull him into my body. My hand grips his ass, and I grind my erection into him. I don't even need the foreplay right now, I'm that damn hard. His lips slowly trail over the skin on my neck, and I hear his whisper. "Your place or mine?"

I pull back enough to tell him his place before I crush my mouth down onto his. His mouth is rough against mine, we are both panting by the time we pull away. He grabs my hand and leads me through the crowd and towards the door, drinks long forgotten. Before he can walk towards a Chevy truck, I stop him and pull him back to me. My hands run up his back, and I claim his mouth with mine again. My tongue slips into his mouth, I massage his tongue with mine until his hands are digging into my back.

When we break apart this time, I can feel his hardness through his jeans. Running my hands down his back, I grip his ass and grind him against me again. "Fuck," I groan. He nips at my bottom lip and pulls it between his teeth.

"You have me so hard right now." He mumbles as he releases my lip.

"Good," I say before I press his body into the wall of the bar. My hand goes to his throat, and I kiss him again. Fuck, I could get used to the way he tastes. The taste of whiskey is like second nature to me; I love the way it mixes with his particular taste.

"We need to get out of here before I fuck you against this wall," I say against his lips. I release my hold on him and watch as he walks towards his truck. When he gives me a questioning look, I nod my head towards my bike. "I'll follow you." He gets in and starts his truck as I start to make my way towards my bike.

Checking the message from River, I see that she's butt hurt about my brother again. She's been trying to get him to notice her but has failed miserably because he thinks I'm fucking her. Sebastian is a loyal son of a bitch, he would never try and steal the girl I'm fucking even if he had feelings for her. I tried to tell him that it wasn't like that between us, but he doesn't believe it.

Putting my phone away, I straddle my bike and turn the key. Listening to her engine roar, I adjust my hard on and motion for him to take off. I follow behind him for the ten miles it takes to get to his place and watch as he pulls in the drive of a small house on the outskirts of this small podunk town. He gets out just as I pull into his drive and park my bike in front of his truck. I don't know what this town's crime rate is, but I'm not taking any chances on my baby.

"Nice bike." He says as I kill the engine.

"Thanks. I custom built her when I turned eighteen." I run my hand over the gas tank, and he makes his way towards me. His eyes never leave mine as he reaches out and pulls my head to his mouth.

"I've always wanted to ride on one of these Harley's." He says when he releases my mouth. My hand grips his hip, I pull him closer and motion for him to get on. He slowly puts his leg over the bike and sits in front of me. My dick is straining against my jean, I want so bad to free the fucker just so I can get his sweet

lips wrapped around me.

"I'll give you something to ride." I murmur, pulling his head to mine. I grip the nape of his hair and run my mouth against his throat. I hear a car coming down the street, but his truck is blocking the sight of us. The lights illuminate the area around us, and when I look down, I can see the bulge in his jeans. My free hand runs down his neck and towards his stomach, slowly feeling my way down his rigid body. When I come to his dick, I rub my hand slowly along his shaft.

He moans in appreciation, and I brace the bike leaning him backward. I run my hands down his chest, and his hands go to the handle bars almost like he's afraid to fall. "I won't let you fall," I say looking up at him. He grins back at me, and I run my hand up his shirt, pulling it up as I go. Kissing my way up his stomach and then back down to the top of his jean, I run a hand down his thigh while the other is rubbing against his jean covered dick.

One of his hands grabs my hair, and he gives it a tug, drawing a groan from deep in my throat. Running my tongue along his skin, I hear his moan. Undoing the button on his jeans, I start to slide down his zipper. Reaching a hand inside, I grip his dick, stroking him slowly. His back arches off the bike and I have to steady us. Leaning my body over his, I run my lips over his skin again and pull his dick out of his jeans. Making my way back down his abs and towards his dick, I hear his intake of breath.

I stroke my hand up and down his shaft a few times; I look up at him to see him watching me intently. His mouth opens as I lower my head and take his tip into my mouth. "Fuck," he gasps. His hand grips my hair tighter as I take him into my mouth as he sets the pace. Pleasuring him the way I like it done to me, I grip his dick tight and swirl my tongue around his head a few times before I take him to the back of my throat.

"Fuck. Your mouth feels so damn good." He thrusts his

hips up and into my mouth. I have to widen my stance even further to keep us from falling over. I suck him until he's good and hard, massaging his balls for a few minutes before I pull him up and kiss his mouth again.

Fuck. I could get lost in his body, and I haven't even seen the whole damn thing yet. His fingers tangle into my hair, I let him control the kiss this time. Cupping his cheek, I let him show me just how he kisses. "I want to suck your dick. If it's as big…" he trails off and runs his hand along my shaft. "Fuck, you feel big." His finger runs along the piercing at the tip of my dick, and I groan.

"Then why don't you take me inside and suck it?" I ask in a husky tone. He leans forward and claims my mouth again before he throws his leg over the bike and makes his way towards the door. Putting my kickstand down, I make sure my vest is still tucked into my bag. I'm not even supposed to go into a bar without my colors on, but I know that shit doesn't fly at the gay bars, so I respect it. If my family found out I wasn't wearing my colors, they'd have my ass. They'd say I was disrespecting the club, the family.

Bikers aren't gay. They are men who fuck woman after woman until there are none left that they haven't fucked. Trust me, I know. My brothers have fucked more women than I can count, they don't even have to chase them. Bitches just flock to those fuckers. Hell, they even flock to me.

Walking towards the door where I see Spencer standing, I have to adjust myself. My dick is pressing against my zipper, and fuck it's uncomfortable. I unbutton my jeans and put my hand inside, slowly stroking myself as I walk towards him.

CHAPTER TWO

The way his eyes are eating me up, tells me all I need to know. I don't typically do one night stands, but there is something about him. Shit, I still don't even know his name. Part of me doesn't even care. The only thing I care about right now is getting him inside and pulling his dick out of his jeans. I want to see if his dick is as big as he feels.

He stalks towards me slowly stroking himself inside of his jeans. I hear a moan slip out of my mouth as I watch him. When he reaches me, he pushes me backward and into the house. My brain isn't functioning, the only thing I can focus on is the look on his face as he scans over my body again. His booted foot kicks my door closed with a loud bang.

Our bodies are so tightly together that I can feel his hand as it rubs up and down his shaft. His other hand comes around and wraps around my neck, pulling me even closer to him. His mouth is a whisper away, and something pulls me to him. I don't know what it is, but I want to do so much to his body.

Closing the distance between us, I kiss him roughly. His fingers tangle into the nape of my hair as my hands grip his back through his tight tee shirt. One of my hands goes to the back of his neck, and I pull his mouth into mine. My tongue slips into his mouth, and our tongues dance together like we've been doing it for years.

Running my hands down his back, I grip the bottom of his tee shirt and slowly pull it up. Every kiss gets hotter, fuck I'm getting harder by the second. Pulling his shirt over his head, I drop it behind us and then look down at his hand that is still stroking himself. Reaching for his jeans, I undo them the rest of the way and start to slide them down his thighs.

His strong, powerful thighs are a fucking sight of beauty. I work with some pretty fit men and not one of them has a body like his. Before I have a chance to sink down to my knees, he stops me and pulls me to his body. His hand releases his dick, and he grabs the bottom of my shirt, pulling it over my head. After he tosses it on the ground, his mouth skims over my skin, and his tongue finds my nipple ring.

Closing my eyes, I let out a low moan. Fuck his mouth feels amazing. "I love these." He whispers against my skin. My hand runs over the back of his brown hair and down his body, straight to his dick. Taking him into my hand, I stroke him a few times before I run my fingers along the tip. Feeling his piercing, I can't help but get excited.

Going to my knees, I caress him a few more times before I take him into my mouth. Swirling my tongue along his piercing, I tease him a little before I use my hand to stroke him in time with my mouth. His hand goes to the back of my head, and he starts to fuck my mouth. Every thrust he makes goes to the back of my throat, I take him in as best as I can. He's bigger than most of the men I've been with over the years, but that doesn't keep me from sucking his dick.

Grabbing his ass, I let him take total control and fuck if it

doesn't turn me on even more. His grunts and moans fill the room, my dick hardens even further in my jeans.

Releasing his ass, I run my hand down my body and tweak my nipples a little before one of my hands slides down my body and to my jeans. Unbuttoning my jeans, I slide them down a little and start to work my own length. His hands grip my hair harder, and he pulls up. I start to stand, and he kisses me deeply. Our mouths battle for dominance and his wins. I bite his lip and tug when he starts to break the kiss.

"As much as I love your mouth on my dick, I need to taste you." My skin breaks out in goosebumps as I watch him drop to his knees and take me into his mouth. He slowly licks my length from the tip to my balls before he goes back to the tip and sucks it into his mouth.

"Oh fuck," I moan. His mouth feels fucking amazing as it slides up and down my cock. When he looks up at me with my dick still in his mouth, I have to think about something other than his beautiful mouth on me. My grandma. Shit, that's gross. She's the nicest old lady, but sometimes she smells like she bathed in a damn candle. That does it.

He continues to work me over and my hand's fist in his hair. I fuck his mouth for a minute before he pulls away and spins me around, pushing me into the door. My hands catch me, and he uses one of his hands to push my back down. My ass is now in his face, and when I look over my shoulder, I can see the lust in his eyes.

The minute his tongue probes my ass, I freeze. My whole body tenses, I try my best to relax. He takes his time working his tongue into my ass, and then he adds a finger. My body is more than willing to take everything he's giving me now, fuck it feels good. Grabbing my dick, I start to stroke myself. "Fuck, babe. That feels so damn good," I moan.

"You like when I fuck you with my fingers?" I moan out a yes in response and press my ass back into his face a little more. I hear my phone ring from my pocket, and I groan out in dissatisfaction. The only reason the ringtone would be going off is because we have a case. Fuck.

I try to stand up, but he doesn't let me. Instead, he stands up and leans his body over mine. My phone stops ringing and then starts again. I hear him groan when it doesn't stop ringing, I put my head against the door. "Sorry, it's work. I need to get it." I say sounding extremely frustrated. He lets me up, and I walk over to my phone that's on the floor. I see my boss' name on the screen, and when I answer it, he barks out my orders.

My hand goes to the bridge of my nose, and I squeeze it. "Yeah, I'm on my way," I sigh. I look over at the sexy biker, but I can't decipher his expression. Once I hang up, I walk back towards him and pull his body into mine. "I'm sorry..." Before I can say anything else, he silences me by crushing his mouth to mine. He grabs my phone out of my hand and starts to push some buttons before handing it back to me.

"I get it. I have times where that shit happens to me. Just give me a ring when you are free." He gives me a devious grin and pulls me in for one more heart-stopping kiss.

When we pull apart, I'm a little speechless. Most men wouldn't give me the time a day after I get called away right before we get to fuck. "You mean that this doesn't turn you off?" I ask with an eyebrow raised.

He shrugs. "It's not that big of a deal. I'll just have fuckin' blue balls like a motherfucker. Nothing I can't handle." Before he can pull away from me, I wrap my fingers around his dick and start to stroke him.

"We can't have that. I'll get you off. Don't want you in pain."

He grins at me, and I sink back down to my knees. I take him into my mouth, I can feel the cold silver jewelry from his Prince Albert piercing glide across my tongue. Taking him as far into my mouth as I can, I slowly start to massage his balls, and his hand creeps up my neck and to my cheek where he cups the side of my face. Looking up at him as I continue to bob on his dick, I see the burning desire in his eyes. His hand moves to my head after a few seconds and then starts to control our pace. He holds my head still and starts to thrust his hips, fucking my mouth the way he likes it.

His dick goes to the back of my throat, I can't help but groan around his thick shaft. Every thrust of his hips brings him closer to his orgasm, and it makes me hot. Watching the pleasure written all over his face gets me gripping my cock. Sliding a hand up and down my shaft, I feel the tightening of my stomach muscles. Fuck. I feel his dick swell in my mouth, and I run my tongue on the underside of his shaft, causing him to grip my hair and give it a rough tug.

I'm so fucking worked up now that I can feel my orgasm just on the brink. When his cum fills my mouth, I feel the warm semen start to squirt onto my belly and hand. Fuck, he's beautiful when he has his head thrown back in pleasure. My eyes can't seem to leave him, I want nothing more than to let him fuck me hard.

As he comes down from his orgasm, he continues to lightly thrust in and out of my mouth until he rides it out completely. Sucking him clean, I release him with a pop, and he grabs my arm, pulling me up his body. His lips land on mine and he pulls me in for a delicious kiss. Every nerve ending comes alive, I want more of him. One night will never be enough.

"Fuck Spencer." He groans against my mouth. "Your mouth is a fuckin' sin." I hear my phone beep again, and I groan. Fucking work always gets in the way of every damn thing. His hand runs down my stomach and through my semen. "I loved watching you come." He whispers in a husky voice. I kiss him once more before I pull back and look at him in the eyes.

"I really have to go." I murmur. He nods his head and pulls me in for one last kiss. He runs his finger through my semen once more when he pulls away and sucks his finger into his mouth. "Goddamn." I moan. He grins at me and pulls his jeans up without another sound. I don't know what the hell I did to deserve a sexy as fuck man dropped in my lap tonight, but I know for sure that I would do it over and over again if I got him as a reward.

We dress in silence, but I can feel his eyes on me every second. When he's dressed, he leans against the wall and just watches me. Grabbing my go bag from the entry way, I walk back over to him. "I'll call you when I get back. Probably be a day or two."

He nods, and I lead him out to the front door. Opening it, I watch the way his ass moves in those tight dark washed jeans. When he gets to his bike, he turns and winks at me. He isn't much for words it seems. I watch him as he straddles the bike and starts the engine. My eyes stay with him until he takes off into the night.

Fuck me. I don't even know what to think. Locking the door, I make my way to my truck and get in. I'll definitely be calling him as soon as we hit the ground again.

CHAPTER THREE

Elijah

By the time I get back to the outskirts of Las Vegas, I decided on heading over to River's place. She wanted to bitch at me anyways about my moron of a brother, so I might as well just grace her with my presence instead. Maybe she'll at least have some alcohol in the cabinet.

Shit after the way Spencer sucked my dick, I need to take the edge off. I wanted to bend him over a damn couch and fuck his ass, but duty calls. As shitty as it is, I get it. I end up doing the same shit every time one of my brother's calls. My loyalties will always lie with the club, and that won't change.

Pulling up to her house, I park my bike and get off. I can still feel the way his tongue felt as it ran along my piercing and shaft. Before I can even knock, the door is thrown open, and I see a pissed off River. "So you just ignore my 911 text messages and show up here. I swear you are worse than your brother." She snaps. I walk over to her and pull her to me.

"Yeah, but you still like me better sweetheart." I kiss her cheek, and the anger disappears. She tries to be a hard-ass, but it's just not her style.

"Where the hell were you? You were supposed to come by hours ago." She looks up at me with a pout, and I shrug.

"I was out," I say, moving past her and into her house.

"Out as in with someone or trolling?" She asks as she shuts the door. My phone beeps, I pull it out to see a text message from Seb. Great. I get to hear it from both sides now.

"Both," I say distractedly.

"Oooh!" she says giddily. "Was it good?" River loves hearing the details of my sex life for some odd reason. She loves hearing about when I fuck them. Her gay porn addiction is kind of frightening, but I just go with it. "Please tell me it wasn't with that douche bag that you were fucking before."

I snort at her statement. "No, it wasn't him. I didn't get a chance to fuck this one. He got called into work. But he does suck dick like a fuckin' dream." She sighs and flops her ass on the couch, looking over at me with this stupid grin.

"You know you should really stop living vicariously through me and man the fuck up and tell Sebastian how you feel." She frowns and shakes her head.

"Please. He still thinks I'm fucking you. When I saw him out tonight, he got all pissy. He didn't like that I was dancing with some loser as he put it when I had you." She wrinkles her nose at me and then throws her head back. "Fuck Seb. I'm done trying to get him to notice me."

I take a seat next to her, and she puts her head on my shoulder. "Are you ever going to tell them?" She asks, running a finger along my thigh.

"I don't know." I blow out a breath and kiss the top of her head. She knows why I don't tell them. I've told her before that

bikers just aren't gay, especially in an MC.

"Your family loves you. Them knowing won't change that Eli."

"They will probably always love me, but things would be different after they find out. I'm not sure I can take the ignorant remarks from the rest of the brothers. They aren't my family, so they don't have to accept it." She gives me a sad smile because she knows it's the truth. River has been to many family barbecues. She knows exactly the type of men they are. They don't hold their opinions back, and I don't expect them to. A lot of them will probably want me out if I outed myself.

Instead of continuing to ask about when I'm going to tell my family that I'm gay, she moves on to the guy from tonight. "So what does this man look like?" She waggles her eyebrows at me, and I shake my head at her. I'm going to need some alcohol for this shit.

"Go get me a beer and I'll tell you." She gives me the stink eye that I've gotten a lot over the years when I don't tell her the information she wants right away. I like to make her work for it.

I watch River get off the couch dramatically and sulk all the way to the kitchen. When she comes back with two beers, I watch her sit down and get comfortable before she faces me and waits expectantly. I swear sometimes she's worse than having a little sister. Not that I would know since I'm the youngest of four boys, but I was around when Anslie was a teenager and let's just say she kept my brother Brantley on his toes. He was always getting pissy when she would date other guys or when she and Casey were at parties getting drunk.

I still remember when he called me to come with him to pick their drunk asses up. Riding with a drunk bitch wasn't something that I had ever wanted to do, yet when he called, I came. No questions asked.

"So?" She asks, poking my arm.

"So what?" I ask. She punches me in the arm, I can't help but laugh at her. It's so damn easy to piss her off sometimes.

"Just fucking tell me Eli or I'll..." She pauses, trying to think of something clever I'm sure.

"Or you'll what?" I ask with a raised eyebrow.

She frowns and then her eyes light up like she figured something out. "I'll tell Candy how much you want to fuck her." I groan at that. I wouldn't touch that bitch even if I was straight. She's the biggest slut we have at the club house and is always hitting on my brothers and I. I'm pretty sure Seb has taken her to bed a few times, but I don't mention that to River. It would probably crush her.

Before I can tell her about Spencer, my phone starts to ring. Looking at the screen, I see Seb's name. I turn the screen towards her, and she grabs it out of my hand and hits the answer button. "Hey Seb," she all but purrs at him. I shake my head at her, and she smacks me.

I pull it away from her and put it on speaker phone. "Hey, darlin' where is my brother?" She giggles and then gives him an answer that I can tell he doesn't like.

"He's a little busy. I have his mouth preoccupied." I hear him growl over the line and her eyes light up. I roll my eyes at them and then she looks back at the phone like she can see him. "What did you need him for?" Her voice is sticky sweet, I know that probably only adds to his anger. He wants her, I know he does. Why he doesn't say anything or try to stake his claim is beyond me.

"Tell him to call me when you two are done fucking around." he bites out.

She doesn't like his shitty attitude typically, I can see that she's going to say something that will probably piss him off more. "We aren't fucking around you asshole. I don't know why you don't listen to us. We are drinking beers and sitting on my couch. Pull that stick out of your ass every once in a while." She huffs out and gets up off the couch. She tosses my phone at me and stalks towards her bedroom. Sighing, I take the phone off speaker and ask him what his problem is.

"I don't fucking know. She drives me fucking insane and when I saw her tonight..." he trails off, and I run my hand over my face. Fuck. I hate being in the middle of this shit.

"Then why the fuck haven't you made a move?" I ask. I don't understand them at all.

"Because she's your girl," he says on a groan. "You know I wouldn't do that shit to you." I can't help but laugh. I don't know how many times I'm going to have to tell this fucker that River and I aren't together.

"Pull your head out of your ass and just fucking date her. She's been in love with you for years. Me and her are never going to get together. I don't know how many times I have to tell you that." My phone beeps in my ear and I pull it away to look at it, I see an unknown number. Instead of checking it, I focus on trying to get Seb to man the fuck up.

"Mom would flip if I went after River." He's got a good point. Mom loves River like a daughter. She always fusses over her and Anslie. Sometimes I think she likes the girls more than us, not that I complain. It just means that she stays out of our business more. The girls are more like a buffer. They keep my mom off my back when I don't want to answer my mom's questions about when River and I are going to have some kids or something stupid like getting married.

I already know that shit isn't in the cards for me. She doesn't take no for an answer, especially since B already has two kids and my mom is ready for more grandkids. Hell, even with Brent having another on the way, my mom still isn't happy. Plus with Jase and his ole' lady's niece that they are adopting, you would think she has enough to do with grandkids, but nope.

"Yeah, but you rather be miserable thinking I'm fucking her or who the fuck knows who else? She said you got all pissy at her tonight cause she was dancing with some douche bag." I hear him groan and then the music in the background gets louder.

"Hey, Seb." Some chick purrs into the phone. He mumbles something, and then he tells me he needed to go, so I just hang up. He gets pissed when it comes to someone touching her, but he still fucks other bitches. I don't understand that idiot sometimes. Checking the message, I can tell that it's Spencer. He must have found what I programmed my number under.

Unknown: *Cute name.*

Me: *I thought you'd like that.*

I walk towards River's room staring at the screen still. When his reply is almost instant, I can feel a rush of excitement. I don't know what it is about him.

Unknown: *It fits you. So I'm on a plane right now, going to New Jersey. Not sure I'll be back in two days like I thought.*

"What's with the frown?" River asks as I make my way towards her bed.

"Oh, uhh…" I pause, looking up at her.

"Are you texting him?" Her voice turns from depressed to excited in an instant.

"He is on a plane to New Jersey right now." She frowns and then pulls me onto the bed with her. We lay side by side in silence for twenty minutes.

"Did you write him back?" She asks when she gets bored of staring at the ceiling.

"No. I'm not desperate," I reply. I turn to look at her, and she nudges me with her arm.

"I never said you were. But don't you want to find love?" her question puts me on the defensive for some reason, and I don't know why.

"How can a one night stand from a bar be love?" I can see her flinch and I feel bad. "I'm sorry River. You know I don't mean it. I love you." She doesn't say anything, and I can tell I pissed her off, I don't ask anything more. Instead, I write Spencer back.

Me: **Too bad. I was hoping to get you alone again soon.**

I feel her head on my shoulder, I know she's reading my messages. "You're message sounds like something I would say to Seb if he ever paid attention to me." I kiss the top of her head, and she just continues to read our exchange.

Unknown: **I'll make it up to you when I get back.**

River takes my phone from me and writes out a message that she won't let me read. I swear she's like a girl starved of her porn tonight.

When my phone dings again, I see a grin appear on her face, and she squeals. I have to rub my ear from the loud ass fucking noise she just made. Holy fuck she's loud. She shows me the screen, and it's a picture. The photo starts at the bottom of his nose. His bright smile is on full display, as are his pecs, perfect fucking abs and the V the dips into the sweats he's wearing in the photo. "Oh shit. Please tell me that he really looks like this with his clothes off," she breathes.

I nod my head at her, and she squeals again. "I fuckin' know why my brother doesn't want your ass now." I cover my ears, and she punches me in the chest. Shit. That fuckin' hurt. She pouts, and I wrap my arm around her, pulling her onto my chest. "Don't get pissy with me." She tries to push away, but I don't let her move. "Yeah sweetheart, that's what he looks like." She starts to type something else on my phone, and I just shake my head at her. She's fucking lucky I love her.

"Is his face as fucking hot as his body?" I nod my head but don't say anything else. Instead, I just close my eyes and listen to her every few minutes send him another message. If shit with him doesn't work out, I'll be blaming her ass for it.

CHAPTER FOUR

Once I finally made it to the office, I got pulled into a briefing. Our new case was a rash of murders through the state of New Jersey. I watched Milli on autopilot as she gave us the details that were provided by the local leos. As much as I was anxious for the new case, I hoped that it was local so I could call the biker from earlier. Shit. I still don't even know his name.

"Three women were found murdered in their apartments on Friday night. Saturday mornings, the calls came in for all three cases. The women's boyfriends were the ones to call 911." Milli states. She pulls the crime scene photos up on the board, and we all stare at them.

As much as I love my job, seeing some of this shit gets tiring. People are all sorts of fucked up and do some unspeakable things for God knows what reason. Ligature marks on each of the victim's necks suggest strangulation.

"What do you guys see?" Dixon, our team chief asks from the head of the table. I've been part of this crime task force for the last three years and have worked my ass off to not be just the gay guy on the team. Yeah, we've had our problems when I first got drafted, but since I proved myself worthy of being part of the team, the guys haven't treated me any different than the rest of them.

We are all good at our jobs, but there have been times where we all don't see eye to eye. Something every team goes through, I'm sure. It could have been because I was new and didn't have the experience most of the team had. I have a degree in psychology. I wasn't in the bureau long before I got moved into the unit.

Canaan and Fox both stare intently at the pictures on the screen before Fox finally says something. "The boyfriends weren't live-ins?"

Milli shakes her head no, and then pulls up a report. "Joshua Michelson called in the murder around eight thirty in the morning when he stopped by to take the victim, Sofie Vargas out for breakfast. He let himself in with the key she gave him. The rest of the statements are similar, just different reasons for the boyfriends to be at the apartments."

A few more ideas are thrown around the table before Dixon finally tells us to grab our bags and head for the plane.

Making my way towards the plane, I scroll through my phone to find the bikers number. I find a contact called 'Your Sexy Biker' and I can't help but grin. A hand hits me on the shoulder, I look over at Canaan, and he's looking over at my phone.

"Sexy biker, huh?" He gives me his cheeky grin, and I just turn the screen off.

"He programmed it in my phone with that name." My lips turn up into a small grin, and he pushes at my shoulder.

"Is that what you were pulled from tonight for the case?" He asks sounding genuinely interested.

"Yeah. We were just getting to the good part." I grin. Canaan smirks at me. He's never been judgmental about my lifestyle. Ever since I came clean with him, he's done nothing but support me. Every once in a while we head out to the bars together and point out the prospects for each other.

"Fuck man. I swear you pull more ass than I do." He says putting his hand on my shoulder.

"It's the pretty face and big dick." I grin. He shakes his head and starts to laugh.

"Shit. I've seen your junk and I have a bigger dick than you so it can't be that." He starts to laugh just as Fox comes up behind me.

"What the fuck are you two gabbing about like a bunch of damn girls?" Fox asks as we get to the plane and take our seats.

"Rico over here was about to get busy with a biker before we got the call." Canaan does this little hip grind thing that makes me laugh at him. He's a cool dude and is only serious when we are working the case.

"Shit. That is the only shitty thing about our jobs. Every time I'm about to get laid the boss man calls." He groans and leans his head back against the seat. He must have been in the same boat as me.

"True," Canaan says with a grin. Before he can say anything else, Dixon walks on board. He scans the plane, taking inventory of us before telling the pilot that we are cleared for take-off. Dixon takes his seat and then starts to read over the file again.

Grabbing my copy of the file, I start to read the interviews with the boyfriends. Everyone is pretty much the same, and that strikes me as strange. The only differences are the reason for the boyfriends to find their girlfriends. One was because he was taking her to breakfast, another was picking her up for work, and the final one was he was just getting back from being out of town.

"Do you guys find it weird that all the boyfriends have pretty much the same story of how they found their girlfriends?" I ask.

"Yeah. You think that maybe they are involved somehow?" Canaan asks.

"Do they have any trails that lead to one another?" Dixon asks. He grabs his phone and calls Milli, putting it on speakerphone. "Hey, Milli, can you check the phone records for all of the victim's boyfriends? See if they knew each other prior to the murders."

"I'll check now. Let me call you back with the results." She chirps into the phone. He hangs up and looks over the crime scene photos again.

"All the murders are slightly different. One was at close range, the second was further away, and the third was shot in the back of her head." He states, handing the photos over to Fox.

Fox stares at them for a long while before he says anything. "The bullet holes are different in each victim. I'm thinking that a different gun was used in each murder."

I nod and try to formulate the scenes in my head. We spend the next hour running through possible scenarios before Dixon tells us to rest up for when we land. We always hit the ground running when we get to a crime scene. It's the same every case, only the cases are different.

Pulling my phone out of my pocket, I turn the screen on to see that it's still on the 'Your Sexy Biker' contact. Hitting the message button, I type out a message to him. The best thing about our private plane is the wifi. We can pretty much call and

text over it with certain internet programs.

Me: ***Cute name.***

Your Sexy Biker: ***I thought you'd like that.***

His reply doesn't take long, and it thrills me that he is even writing back after I had to leave right before we got to the good part.

Me: ***It fits you. So I'm on a plane right now, going to New Jersey. Not sure I'll be back in two days like I thought.***

Your Sexy Biker: ***Too bad. I was hoping to get you alone again soon.***

My dick twitches in my jeans and damn if that is the only thing I can now think about. Before I can write back, I see Canaan grinning at me. Sometimes I don't even know why we are friends. He gets up from where he's sitting and takes a seat next to me. "You texting your sexy biker?" he grins, and I go back to texting with the biker.

Me: ***I'll make it up to you when I get back.***

The grin on my face gives me away, and Canaan keeps trying to get me to give him something, but I don't give him anything. I just keep on writing him back. The next text message that comes in shocks me. It doesn't seem like something he'd ask, but when I look at Canaan, he reads the message over my shoulder and nods his head.

Your Sexy Biker: ***I need a picture to remember you by while you're gone.***

Canaan waggles his eyebrows at me, and I have to push him away from me. "You really need a better sex life if you are this fascinated in mine." He grabs my phone from me and taps the photos icon before scrolling along to find something to send him. Before I can even see the photo he's about to send, he hits the button and grins back at me. I grab my phone from him and see the photo he just sent to the biker.

I groan and cover my face with my arm, leaning back on the chair. "Fuck. Seriously? You sent him that one?" That photo was one I took when I was fucking around one night. I had just finished working out at the gym and felt like taking a selfie. I feel my phone vibrate again and open the new message.

Your Sexy Biker: *Damn, you have no idea what I want to do to you.*

Me: *If it's anything like earlier, I can't wait to find out.*

Your Sexy Biker: *It will be even better.*

Me*: Do I get a photo of you too?*

Canaan closes his eyes next to me, and I wait for the next message. I feel my phone vibrate again and when I look down at the screen, I can feel my heart start to race as my finger hovers over the text. Opening the message, I see the picture he sent. Holy fuck. I can feel my jeans tighten and when I feel Canaan move closer to me, I turn the screen off.

"That him?" He asks over my shoulder.

"Yeah." It doesn't show his face, just like my photo. I can see his tattoos on display, and it actually looks like someone else took the photo of him. My eyes follow the path down his chest to the V that disappears into his jeans that are low on his narrow hips. "Damn," I whisper.

"He's got some nice ink," Canaan says, before leaning back and resting his head against the chair he's sitting on. I write him back quickly before I shut my phone off. I need to get a nap in

before we land, or I'll be a walking zombie.

Me: *I don't know how I'm going to work with the hard on I now have. I have to get back to work. I'll call you when I get a chance.*

His response is quick, and it makes me smile.

Your Sexy Biker: *I did my job then. I'll talk to you later.*

Closing my eyes, I try like hell to fall asleep, but it never happens. I end up just thinking about tonight and how it ended. My eyes open and I see Dixon reading over the case files still. Getting up from my seat, I make my way over to the table he's sitting at.

"You see something we've missed so far?" He shrugs his shoulder, and I grab one of the files.

"Nothing yet. The boyfriend's stories don't make a lot of sense and seem too fucking similar. The murders are a month apart, and I just can't figure it out," he rubs his eyes and pinches the bridge of his nose.

"You think the boyfriends are connected," I state. I run my eyes over the crime scene photos once more, and I notice a photo in the background. I set the photo down and point at the photo. Dixon takes the photo and stares at it for a second before I look at the next case's crime scene photo. I noticed another photo in that photo. I don't see the man in the photo, but I do see the victim and part of someone's arm. The arm has a tattoo on it, and it looks similar to the man from the first photo. The third is the same, but maybe there is something about that similar looking tattoo.

CHAPTER FIVE

Elijah

Rolling over, I see River's closed eyes lying next to me. We got drunk last night, and there was no fucking way I was driving home. Slipping out of bed, I make my way to the bathroom to take a piss. My head is fucking pounding, that is the last time I let her talk me into drinking wine when the beer is all fucking gone.

My phone starts to ring loudly. When I look over my shoulder, I groan, and then I hear River's bitching. She yells at me from the bed, and I can't help but grin. That's what she gets. "I swear to God if you don't answer your damn phone, I'll kill you." I chuckle at her and flush the toilet. Walking towards the bed, I watch in amusement as she throws the phone at me.

Catching it, I look at the screen and see my brother's name. "What B?" I groan into the phone. River puts the pillow over her head, and I walk over to her and pull it off. Pressing a kiss to the side of her head, I whisper that I'll call her later. Instead of answering, she just pulls the pillow back over her head muttering something.

Walking out the door, I listen to Brant bitching about something. "Dude you sound like a fucking bitch." He continues to go on about how Anslie's a bitch and blah, blah, blah. Fuck, I

40

could care less what his problems are with his ole' lady. He and Jase are the ones that typically talk to each other about this shit. Hell, they both live that shit. Why the fuck didn't he call his twin?

"Fuck you. I'm going to laugh my damn ass off when you meet your damn match, and she grabs you by the balls." I snort at that as I pull out a cigarette from the pack I have stashed away in my bags. Lighting it up, I lean against my bike and listen to the rest of his bitching. The sooner he gets it out, the sooner I get to go home and shower.

"I still don't get what the fuck you keep her around for if all you do is bitch." I blow out a cloud of smoke and shut my eyes. The sun feels fucking amazing on my skin right now, I would much rather be on the road, curving around turns on my Harley, heading towards the mountains. The reason I love Las Vegas is because of the hot sun, long winding roads and the mountains in the distance.

"Are you even fucking listening to me?" he finally asks.

"No," I answer honestly, because fuck, I could care less what his and Anslie's issues are. I love the girl to death, and I love my brother, but I don't care. I've got my own shit to worry about.

"Fuck you, Eli. Of course you're not." He sighs into the phone. "Can you come watch the twins while I take Anslie out? Only a few hours." I laugh at him this time. After spending all that time bitching, he wants to take her out.

"You make no fucking sense half the time. You were just bitching about Anslie, and now you want to take her out?" Opening my eyes, I pull the phone away from my ear for a second so I can check the time. Six fucking twenty in the morning and he's already asking favors. Fuck me.

"She's it for me. As pissed off as she makes me, I wouldn't

trade her for anyone." I want to gag at that shit. Seriously why does he have to go and say mushy shit?

"Can I at least shower first? I haven't even made it back to the clubhouse." I hear his laugh before he tells me to come by in two hours. It will give them time to feed the twins before I get there. Pocketing my phone before he can con me into doing something else today, I straddle my bike and put my cigarette out on the bottom of my boot. Putting the butt into my pocket, I start the engine and let it idle for a minute before I take off.

One thing my mom hated when she did my laundry as I got older was when I would leave cigarette butts in my pockets. She would bitch at me for it, but I hate leaving them on the ground, it was the only other place I could stash them. Now the prospects get to deal with them.

As I pull up to the clubhouse, I see my old man standing off to the side yard. He's looking at something, but I can't tell what it is from where I'm at. Putting my kickstand down, I shut my bike off and dismount it. Walking over towards him, I see what looks like a person laying on the ground. As I get closer, I see blonde hair everywhere.

"What happened?" I ask when I get next to him. He shakes his head and looks over his shoulder when the doors to the clubhouse open.

"What do we have?" Cason, our president, barks out as he makes his way over to us.

"No fucking idea. One of the prospects just came to me saying something about a bitch being outside the doors. I came out here and seen her." My old man runs a hand through his graying hair and looks up towards the sky.

"She looks fucking familiar," I state, leaning down to see her face better.

42

"Like who?" Prez questions.

"Remember that bitch that had Dom's kid?" They both look back over to her, I see Cason pull out his phone and dial a number. A couple months ago, Dom got word that she skipped town while she was out on bail. Maybe she fucked with the wrong person this time. All I know is that she got what she deserved.

"D, I need you here now." He pauses for a second before he says anything else. "I don't give a fuck what you're in the middle of; I need you here right fuckin' now." He hangs up, and I stand up.

"Why the fuck would someone dump her on our doorstep?" my old man asks from beside me.

"No idea," Prez says. He dials another number and when I hear the tone, I know he's talking to Danvers. "I need you to get to the clubhouse, but I want it silent. No radioing it in until we talk." He hangs up again, and I feel my phone vibrate in my pocket. Pulling it out, I see Spencer's name on the screen.

Spencer: *I'm running on fumes right now because I couldn't get your picture out of my mind. We landed three hours ago and we've been on the go since. Shitty.*

I can't help but grin at that. River begged me to send Spencer a photo last night. Hell, she even volunteered to take it for me. She all but pulled my tee shirt off of me and forced me to stand where she wanted and everything. I'm glad to know that her idea made him have a long night thinking about me. If I'm honest, he's pretty much the only thing I could think about too. The alcohol couldn't even keep my mind off him for long.

Before I can type out a message back, I hear a Harley come roaring into the lot behind us. When we all turn, we see Dom getting off his bike and making his way towards us. "This shit better be good," Dom grumbles out. When he comes to a stop next to me, I see his eyes widen with surprise. At least we know he didn't do this.

"What the fuck happened?" His voice is tense, and you would think that he'd be happy that this bitch was dead.

"No idea." My dad states. "I have a prospect getting the tape from last night and this morning, but it had to be after six am. That's when I got here, and that bitch was nowhere in sight." His phone starts to ring, and he answers it walking away.

We stand there staring at the body for a good twenty minutes before Danvers comes up behind us. "What the fuck happened?" He asks, looking between the three of us.

"No fuckin' clue. Haven't looked at the tapes yet." Danvers nods his head and makes his way over to the body. He checks a few things before he looks over his shoulder at us.

"You boys didn't do this shit, did you?" he asks. He takes in her face, I know he's putting together who she is.

"No. We didn't do shit. One of the prospects found her out here." Prez grits out. He's pissed that someone had the balls to toss her on our doorstep. Whoever it is probably knows our relation with her. The prospect comes out with a tablet and brings it over to us. Danvers comes over, and Prez hits the play button. We watch the tapes for a few minutes before we see a couple of men in all black. They look around before dumping the body on the ground. When they turn to walk away, we get a glimpse at one of their faces.

Prez pauses the video and takes a screenshot. He taps at the screen and sends the photo over to Danvers. "I'll start running facial recognition on the photo, and I'll let you know what I find out. I'm going to need to call this shit in now."

44

"Do what you need to. Let me know if you need anything from us." They shake hands, and Danvers walks away to place a call to his department. One good thing about having Danvers on our side is that he doesn't jump to conclusions. He finds the facts before he immediately blames us for shit. Plus he knows we only do what we have to in order to protect our own.

We don't kill women for the hell of it. If anything we protect them even if they don't always deserve it. A few more of the guys start to show up, and everyone's attention is focused on the dead girl. "I need to head out," I state, looking over at my pops and Prez.

"Where the fuck you going?" My dad clips.

"Babysitting for that shithead brother of mine," I state. He nods his head before turning towards Prez.

"We need to call church when we have more info on the fuckers who dropped her here." Prez nods his head and looks back over to me.

"Tell B what is going on and make sure you both are on high alert. I don't want anything else happening." I nod and make my way into the clubhouse to shower.

Once I'm showered and dressed, I make my way out to my bike. Now there are even more brothers gathered around, and I'm actually thankful that I have a date with the coolest little kids I know.

CHAPTER SIX

The time we've interviewed the victims' families, I have a sneaking suspicion that the boyfriends are either the same person or in on it together. Each of the families spoke highly of the boyfriend, yet didn't have photos of their daughter's with the men in question. The only thing that makes sense is that they are in fact the same person.

Taking a seat at the conference table at the station, I start to scan the photos again to see if I missed anything.

"You're going to wear yourself out," Canaan says as he takes a seat next to me. He pulls the photo out of my hand and starts to look at it.

"Naw, I'm good. I'm just trying to link the boyfriend. I think they are all the same guy." I point to the photo, and he looks at it intently. "See this tattoo?" He nods his head, so I grab the next one and point it out on that photo too. "Here it is again." He reaches for the other photo, and it's in that one as well.

"Shit," he breathes. "What is the chance that three men have the same exact tattoo in three different towns?"

"It's very slim," I reply. Not that he really cares the answer. He is thinking the same thing I am now. My phone buzzes with a new message in my pocket. My mind flashes to the biker, but checking the time on my watch, I see that it's a little past midnight there. We've been up for more than twenty-four hours. Rubbing my palms over my eyes, I stifle a yawn and lean back in my chair.

"You going to ignore it?" When I look over at Canaan, he has a grin on his face. "If I had the attention of a hot woman, I definitely wouldn't be ignoring it." I shake my head at him, and he just laughs. We are pretty much the only ones still here in the precinct beside the cops that are on the night shift.

"Let's head out. You can go talk to lover boy at the hotel." I sigh and get up from my seat. As much as I want to talk to the biker, I'm more interested in sleeping. Tomorrow we have an early wake-up call, and I'm already dreading it.

By the time we pull up to the hotel, I'm dragging ass and so is Canaan, I don't have to listen to him telling me to go talk to the biker. I make my way to my room, and he makes his way to his without another word. Closing the door behind me, I pull my phone out and hit the message button.

Seeing his words on my screen, I feel my body heat up. Shit.

Your Sexy Biker: *Tell me you're coming back to town soon.*

I groan and sit on the edge of the bed. My bag is sitting in the corner of the room, but I don't bother moving to it. The only thing I need right now is my phone charger, and I left that at the station.

Me: *Won't know probably until tomorrow. I'm hoping we do though.*

His response is almost instant. Part of me wonders if he was waiting for my message to come through.

My Sexy Biker: *What are you doing right now?*

My dick hardens at his message, and I run my hand on the outline of my dick through my jeans.

Me: *Just got back to my room. You?*

I am playing with fire right now. Part of me wants to continue the messaging and imagining the way his body felt against mine, but the other part of me is exhausted and ready to pass the fuck out. My curiosity wins out like always as I wait impatiently for his next message.

My Sexy Biker: *<picture attachment> Showin' is easier than telling.*

I groan when I click on the photo he sent. *Fuck.* His body is fucking amazing. What I wouldn't give to be able to run my tongue along the contours of his abs. My dick presses against the zipper of my jeans, I can't think of anything but him now.

Me: *Damn. If I could, I'd be on the next plane home.*

My Sexy Biker: *I definitely wouldn't complain about that. I wish your mouth was my hand right now.*

Unbuttoning my jeans, I push them down my hips and stand up to push them the rest of the way down. I start to unbutton my shirt and toss it on the ground. The only thing on my mind right now is imagining him in this room with me. Laying back on the bed, I pull my boxer briefs down enough to get my dick out. My finger runs over the tip, I feel the precum that is already gathering there.

Me: *My dick is hard just thinking about you.*

My Sexy Biker: *I want to see. Show me.*

Fuck it. Hitting a few buttons, I go to the facetime app and hit call on his name. I can feel the nerves take over my body as I wait for him to answer the call. When the screen turns on, I see the outline of his body. The room he is in is dark, with very little light. "Hey." He rasps over the line. His husky voice turns me on more, I have to wrap my fingers around my dick and squeeze.

"Hi." My voice doesn't even sound like mine. "I thought this would be the best way to show you." I can see him scan over my body as I hold the phone above me. His eyes stay on my dick longer than the rest of me, and I can hear his groan through the phone.

"You have no fuckin' clue how much I want you right now." He leaves the screen for a second and then I see his body. The light he turned on shows me everything I've been missing since I was called away to this damn case.

Never have I been this way about a guy I met in a bar. Typically, I could care less if I ever talked to them again even if we didn't have sex. Sometimes when I'm in the bar to get laid, we go back to one of our places and end up just messing around. But with this biker, I want to see him again. Just staring at his body gets me harder than ever before.

There is something about a man with a nipple ring that turns me the fuck on. I didn't notice it the other night. His hand grips his dick, I watch as he strokes himself slowly. His fingers run over his piercing, and I want to wrap my mouth around it again, feel the cold metal in my mouth as I take him to the back of my throat.

"Spencer," he moans. "I want to watch you." I slide my hand down my stomach, stopping my hand at the tip. I swirl my finger around the tip before I grip it tightly and slowly move my hand up and down my shaft. His eyes follow my hand as he continues to stroke himself.

I watch the way his abs constrict as he jerks himself. His powerful forearms flex with every stroke and my God it gets me close. Just the sight of his powerful body gets me hot. My whole body feels like it's about to go up in flames. "I'm going to come," I grit out. My teeth are clenched, and the only thing I can focus on now is his face.

The lust written all over his face is what finally pushes me over the edge. "Oh fuck," he groans. My eyes close, I can hear his heavy breathing through the phone. "I'm going to come." His voice strains and when I open my eyes, I see the spurts of cum as they coat his rock hard stomach.

"That is so fuckin' hot…" I pause. I still don't even know his name. It's not like I'm going to call him my sexy biker like his contact says in my phone.

"Elijah. My name is Elijah," he breaths out. I watch as he strokes himself some more, drawing the last of the cum from his spent cock. Damn, is that a beautiful sight.

"Elijah." I test his name, and I like the way it sounds.

"Fuck, I love the way you say my name. If I'd known it sounded that good from your lips, I would have told you last night." I grin at his words.

"Well, we were a little busy at the time," I smirk. He chuckles, and banging on his door takes his attention away from me.

"Eli, get your ass out here." Watching him, I see his eyes change, and then he sighs.

"I need to get going. I'll give you a call tomorrow." His eyes

move from whatever he's looking at back to me. A small grin pulls at the side of his mouth as he watches me.

"Okay. Have a good night." He winks at me before ending the call. Blowing out a breath, I look at the time and groan. Tomorrow I'm going to need lots of damn coffee to even be able to function. Getting off the bed, I make my way into the shower to wash the cum off my skin. Watching the way his body tensed up as he came was one of the hottest things I've ever witnessed, I can't wait until I can see it again in person.

Once I clean off, I shut the water off, towel dry and make my way to bed. Three hours of sleep is better than none I guess. Slipping under the covers, I look up at the ceiling. Being in hotel rooms is the only thing I hate about this job. The rooms make me feel so damn claustrophobic. I almost didn't even remember that I was here until now. My mind was too focused on what Elijah was doing to pay much attention to my surroundings.

Closing my eyes, I try to push all thoughts of him out of my head so I can finally fall asleep. Just as I'm about to fall asleep, my phone beeps with a new message.

My Sexy Biker: *Dream about me.*

Fuck. I'm totally fucking screwed.

The next morning, I wake up at five a.m. and fumble my way into the shower. Letting the hot water hit my skin, I just stand there until I hear my phone ringing in the other room. I'm tired and in desperate need of coffee before I even think about anything case related. Shutting the water off, I grab a towel and wrap it around my waist before walking over to my phone.

"Hart," I answer right before it goes to voicemail.

"Hey man, you almost ready? We are getting ready to leave." I sigh and run my hand through my wet hair.

"Yeah, I'll be down in a minute. Woke up late. Grab me a coffee?" Canaan chuckles over the line, and I want to punch the asshole.

"Late night talking to your new friend?" I can already imagine him waggling his eyebrows as he asks the question.

"Just get me a coffee. I'll be down in a minute." I state again. I can hear his laugh as he says he will and the line goes dead. Sometimes I don't know why I became friends with him.

Walking over to my bag, I pull out a clean pair of jeans and a dark gray button up shirt. Once I'm dressed, I make my way back into the bathroom to brush my teeth and style my hair a little before grabbing my boots and pulling them on my feet quickly. Making my way down to the lobby as quickly as I can, I see the rest of the guys standing there. They all have coffee in their hands, and they are talking quietly to each other.

"Here," Canaan says pushing a coffee towards me. I take it and sip on the hot liquid. I groan as the liquid hits my tongue, Canaan gives me a knowing grin. Fucker.

"Let's get to the station. We have some leads to follow up on, and I want to interview the boyfriends today." Dixon states. We follow his lead and walk out to our SUV's.

CHAPTER SEVEN

After getting off the phone with Spencer last night, my night went from good to bad in a matter of minutes. Prez decided on sending us on a run that lasted for most of the night. By the time we finally made it back to the clubhouse, it was already morning. Walking through the clubhouse, I make my way to the bar and ask for a shot of whiskey. I'm not even picky as to what the prospect gives me as long as it's something strong.

My body is fucking exhausted, my mind doesn't stray too far from Spencer. Watching him come last night was the damn highlight of my day. With all the shit that's been going on here lately, it's nice to have a distraction. Now only if I can get him to come back to town so I can be buried deep inside of him.

Once I down my shot, my phone starts to ring. "Fuck." I groan. Looking at the screen, I see River's smiling face. As soon as I hit the answer button, I regret it. "Yeah?"

"Oh my God. I'm so glad you're awake. I need your help." I sigh and take a seat back on the bar stool I was just vacating.

"What's up?" I ask, not really wanting to know the answer. I love her and everything, but I'm not really in the mood to listen to her bitch about my brother and how he's still ignoring her.

"My parents are throwing this party, and I need a date. Please tell me you'll come. They will freak out if I show up alone and plus they invited that asshole I used to date. You remember the one I told you about? He's supposedly only going so that he can see me and I don't want to go alone in case he tries to put the moves on me again. Please say you'll come." My head spins with how fast all those fuckin' words just came out of her mouth.

"Seriously? You want me to be your date because you still don't have the balls to ask my brother out?" I groan, putting my head in my hand and leaning against the bar. Sometimes I don't get them. I see the way they both look at the other when they think no one is looking. It's fucking pathetic.

"I swear to God, I will put my heel into your dick if you start with me. I'm panicking here, and you are talking shit." I hear her blow out a breath over the line, I can't help but smirk.

"You won't do shit. When and where?" I finally give in and ask.

"Friday night, seven p.m., at my parents' house, and dress nicely."

"What you don't think I dress nicely?" I joke with her.

"You know I love your badass biker look, but you know my parents." She sighs before she continues. "It's some fancy dinner thing with a few people they are trying to impress." I don't say anything else because I can tell she's already had enough of my shit for one day.

"You don't think Seb would dress nicely for you?" I ask a hint of amusement in my voice.

"If he dressed nice, I might have a heart attack," she

giggles. "He just doesn't do dress pants and button ups. Plus he hates me half the time." Her sigh is loud over the phone. Maybe I can get Seb to stand in for me Friday night.

"Eli don't you dare trick your brother into showing up in your place." I laugh silently and wait for her to continue. I'm sure she's not done bitching at me yet. "I mean it. He isn't invited, and I'll already have enough drama with that guy my parents invited, I don't need his sexy ass pissing me off too."

"So you pretty much want me there to scare the fucker off." I get up from my stool and start to make my way to my room. My one track mind is now focused on showering and heading to bed.

"Yes," she chirps.

"Well, that I can do. Just keep your damn mouth off of me this time. We don't need more people thinking that we are together." She starts to laugh into the phone, and I roll my eyes. She loves to fuck with people for God knows what reason. Everyone that sees us together thinks that we are together and as good as it is to keep my cover, she does nothing for me sexually. On the plus side, she is my best friend.

"Sweetheart, everyone already thinks we are together. Just go with the damn flow." I sigh and run my hand through my long hair. I need to get this shit cut off soon.

"Do I need to shave too?" I ask. When I make it into my room, I head straight for the bathroom and start the shower. While the water warms up, I look at myself in the mirror. I wonder if Spencer likes baby faces or beards. Shit, I seriously need to get my mind off of him.

"Uh, since when do you ask me that? Are you feeling okay or is that new guy messing with your head already?" See, that is why I don't tell her shit. She's always got something stupid to say to me that will more than likely piss me off.

"Fuck off," I say lightly. She starts to giggle, and I curse under my breath.

"He so is!" she squeals. "Oh my God! This is the best thing ever! You've never been hooked on anyone like this before! I want to meet him."

"No. I don't..." I pause. Shit, me and him aren't even together. There is no way I'm subjecting anyone to her crazy ass if I don't have to. "We aren't together, so no." I finally get out.

"Oh boo. You're such a bore. Fine. Friday, don't be late."

"You know I will be," I respond quickly. I hear her huff out, but I end the call before she can start bitching at me. She knows I'm always late, I don't know why she'd even try to tell me to be there on time.

Stripping down and stepping into the shower, I stand under the stream and let the water loosen my tense shoulders. After the prospect found that woman at the clubhouse, we've been under heavy scrutiny. Prez and my old man are both pissed as hell, the only reprieve I was able to have was going on that damn run last night. At least I didn't have to listen to their bitchin' about whoever dumped that whore on our steps.

The cops think we have something to do with that shit, but we don't. The word almost came down to deal with her when she skipped town on her bail, but Dom said no. He didn't want to bring unnecessary heat on us for her death. So we dropped that shit with her and have just been keeping our eyes and ears open in case she came around again. There is no way in hell any of us would let her get close to Axle again.

As soon as I wash my greasy hair and wash my body, I shut the water off and make my way out of the shower. Barely

toweling off before making my way to bed, not bothering to put anything on, I slip under my covers and lay my head against the pillows. My whole body is exhausted, and it doesn't take me long until I'm out.

My phone beeps and I groggily reach for it. When I hit a button and put it to my ear, I don't expect the voice on the other end of the line. "Yeah?" I ask. I cover my eyes with my arm and wait for whoever the fuck it is to say something.

"Hey, Hun. I was wondering if you were free tonight." I roll over to my side and grin.

"Yeah, Mom. I'm free as long as your old man doesn't demand I do another run." I can picture her standing at the stove, making dinner or some sort of cookie that the twins will be demolishing before the rest of us even get a chance to try one.

"Great, can you come by in an hour?" I roll back over to look at the clock and see that it's almost seven. I've slept pretty much the whole damn day away.

"Yeah. Let me wake up a little before I make my way to you." I can practically hear her grin through the phone when she tells me to take my time and that she can't wait to see me.

I don't spend nearly enough time seeing my mom. You would think I did, since I live at the clubhouse and grew up not too far from it. But ever since I decided to stop lying to myself about who I was, I slowly pushed everyone else out of my personal life. The only constant has been River, and that's because she refuses to let me kick her ass to the curb. Trust me, I've tried.

My mom was always my rock, and I hate that I've treated her pretty shitty the last few years. Even when everyone is at family barbecues, I tend to keep to myself. She tries to get me to talk to her, but part of me doesn't know how to be me anymore. Especially with the secret I carry.

Once I get dressed and make my way over to my parent's house, I feel like I'm transported into my sixteen-year-old body. Walking up their steps, I stare at the door and will myself to get out of my own head. I'm not a kid anymore. I'm a grown ass man, and my decisions are my own.

Before I can even put my hand on the doorknob, it opens, and I see my old man's face. "Hey son," he says eyeing me.

"Hey Pop. I'm here to see mom. She inside?" He nods and moves so I can walk past him.

"You coming by the clubhouse later?" He asks, making his way towards his bike. I nod my head and watch him as he gets on the bike and starts the engine. There must be something going on tonight, I am just not privy to the damn information yet.

Closing the door behind me, I make my way towards the kitchen where my mom is standing, doing the dishes. "Hey mom," I greet. I walk over to her and press a kiss on her cheek.

"My baby boy," she grins. I lean against the counter and watch her as she cleans a few more dishes before she rinses her hands and dries them on the towel at her thigh on the cabinet. "So how are things going? I feel like I never see you anymore or you're ignoring me when I do see you." She frowns at me, and I look down at the ground.

"Sweetheart, I'm not trying to give you a hard time, I just want to know what's got you..." She trails off thinking of the right words to say. "I don't know distant maybe? You and I used to be close, but now I see your brothers more than you."

I sigh. I hate hurting my mom's feelings. She's always been the one on my side through everything and over the last few

years, I've cut her out completely. "You know it's nothing like that," I say. She leans against the counter too and watches me. Sometimes I feel like she knows. Maybe if she knew, it would be a little less of a burden that I carry on my shoulders every day. "I just... I don't know. Half the time I don't feel like I belong." I shake my head as I think of the words that just came out of my mouth.

"What do you mean? Why don't you feel like you belong?" Her question isn't hard to answer; it's just hard to get the words out. How do you tell your mom that you're gay? That everything she's known about me for years is a lie to keep people from asking too many questions.

"I don't know. You remember when I was younger and I rather hang with you than my brothers?" She nods her head, and her eyes soften.

"Elijah, I don't want you to ever think you can't tell me whatever it is you're keeping secret. I love you no matter what. You're my son, and that will never change."

"Sometimes it's not that easy," I reply. I feel my phone go off in my pocket, but I don't reach for it. Spending my time here with my mom is right where I need to be right now.

"I won't judge you, sweetheart." Her eyes beg me to tell her my secret. She wants me to trust her enough to tell her, and I want that too. I'm afraid I'll just crush her instead. Ah fuck, here goes nothing.

"You know how everyone thinks River and I are together?" She nods her head, but doesn't interrupt or say anything to keep me from talking. "Well, we aren't. We've never been together. We are purely friends." She nods again, and I blow out a breath before continuing. "Everyone thinks we are together because they never see me with another woman other than her, but they don't see me with women because I'm gay." My eyes meet hers, and I see the tears pooling in them. Her hand goes to her mouth, and she reaches for me.

"My sweet boy." She murmurs before pulling me into her embrace. "I've had a feeling for a long time, but I didn't want to say anything in front of your brothers if I was wrong." I wrap my arms around her small frame and close my eyes. "Don't ever let one of your brothers make you feel less because you don't have the same tastes as them." I smile against her hair, and her grip on me tightens.

When she pulls away, she gives me a glaring look that she used to give us as kids. "Does that mean you'll finally let Seb and River have a shot? They would sure make beautiful babies together." I laugh at her. Of course, that is what she's thinking about.

"Mom, I've been trying to get Seb to date her for years. He thinks he is stepping on my toes or some shit. So unless I come clean to them, I don't see it happening." She sighs and puts her head on my shoulder.

"I know you think they'll judge you, but I know my boys. They will love you no matter what. We are your family, and we will always stand behind you one hundred percent." She doesn't know the shit they say half the time when it's just us hanging around bullshitting. Them finding out isn't something I'm really looking forward to. I might need to be drunk to handle that shit.

I've heard horror stories about the beatings some members of other clubs took when they came out to their brothers. Although I don't think Prez would bring down that ruling, I have a feeling that words will be exchanged and fists will fly.

CHAPTER EIGHT

Spencer

After we spent the whole day tracking down the boyfriends, we finally got them into interview rooms. Although my suspicion about them being the same person was wrong, I got part of it right. They all share the same tattoo. After interviewing them, we learned that they were all part of the same frat back in college.

As I start to connect the dots the best I can, the fact that they know each other stands out to me. What are the chances that three frat brothers lose their girlfriends in almost the same manner within weeks of each other?

"What are you thinking Hart?" Dixon asks from behind me. I'm currently staring at the big white board with all of our timelines and suspects. My eyes trail between all the men and all their alibis. None of them help the other, and they are all weak, to say the least.

"What if this is some sort of pact?" I ask, looking over my shoulder at him. He walks closer, and I hear footsteps behind us, alerting me that Canaan and Fox are probably coming to stand behind me too.

I point to the first murder victim and her boyfriend. "If you look at this boyfriend, you see that he doesn't have an alibi for this murder, but he has one for his girlfriend and the other victim, and vice versa. I point to the ones in the order that they don't make sense.

"So you think that they killed each other's girlfriends? But for what reason?" My phone starts to ring, and when I see the screen, I see Milli's name pop up. I've been waiting for her call. Putting her on speaker phone, I greet her and let her know we are all there with her.

"Hey, guys! I just wanted to let you know about the life insurance policies on each of the women. Spence, you are a genius." I ignore her comment and continue listening. "Each woman had a five hundred thousand dollar policy purchased on them three months before their murders."

"And who are the beneficiaries?" Fox asks.

"The boyfriends. Each woman's boyfriend bought the policy on their girlfriend and named themselves as the beneficiary. Not very sneaky if you ask me," she giggles. This is what I like about Milli, she brings a little bit of happiness to this line of work that is the typical morbid and depressing life we live while on cases.

"Are they still in the interview rooms?" Dixon asks. Canaan nods his head in affirmative.

"Thanks, Milli. We will see you soon." She says her goodbye before I end the call and pocket my phone. I follow the guys towards the interview rooms, and we split up. A detective from the station we are at walks into a room with Dixon, while Canaan and I walk into another room. He tosses the file folder with the life insurance policy for his girlfriend on the table, and we both take a seat in front of the guy.

"Joshua Michelson," Canaan says flipping open the file and looking down at it. "I see you took a life insurance policy out on your girlfriend, Sofie Vargas, three months before her death." I watch the way he sits there in the chair. His eyes move around the small interview room, never looking at us.

"What does that matter? I just wanted her to be protected in case of something." He finally says, not making eye contact with anyone.

"How the fuck does it help her if the policy only pays out if she dies?" Canaan growls. He slams his hands down on the table in front of us, and I watch Joshua's body tighten. He looks over at me, but doesn't say anything. I continue to watch his body language and see that he's starting to sweat. I know he's guilty, but I need to prove it.

"You didn't kill her," I state calmly. Canaan's head snaps in my direction, but I don't look at him. I can feel his anger bouncing around the room. Joshua shakes his head no, but doesn't say the words. He can't.

"But you did kill one of the other girls." I finally add in. He pales before he pushes out of his chair.

"I would never kill her. I loved her." He finally says. His face turns dark when he continues. "But that stupid bitch cheated on me. I had to make her pay. They all need to pay." I look over at Canaan, and he raises an eyebrow at me.

"Why did the others need to pay?" I ask.

"Those bitches weren't any better than Sofie. They were all whores. We did it to teach those stupid bitches a lesson." I feel the anger in me flare up. How the fuck could he have his girlfriend killed over cheating on him. Why not just break up with her if she wasn't faithful?

"I'm going to need you to write down your confession and sign it." I push a pad of paper that I walked in with and a pen in front of him.

"They fucking deserved it." He spits again. It's almost like he's trying to convince himself that what they did was okay. That shit will never be okay.

As he starts to write, Canaan looks over at me, and I shrug. I feel my phone beep in my pocket. Pulling it out, I see a message from Dixon.

Dixon: *You get anything?*

Me: *He's writing out a confession.*

His response is immediate. I'm sure he's going to tell the other boyfriend that Joshua is currently writing a confession, putting the blame on the others in order to get them to confess too.

Dixon: *Good job guys.*

I don't bother writing him back. I close out of the message and see that I have another one in my inbox. Clicking the new message, I see his name show up.

My Sexy Biker: *Please tell me you're coming home soon.*

I stare at his message a little too long because Canaan nudges me with his arm. I look up from the screen just as Joshua is pushing the pad of paper back to me. I pocket my phone, ignoring the words that are now burned into my head.

Good thing we are heading home tonight. Now that we have confessions, we can hand the cases back over to the local leos and they can close them up. After reading over the

confession and how the three old frat buddies decided on coming together to kill each other's girlfriends, I tell him to get up and slap a pair of cuffs on his wrists.

An officer comes into the room and leads him towards booking. As we exit the room, I see the other two boyfriends being led out as well. Fox and Dixon look over at us, and Dixon nods his head. He knows that we don't do this shit for the recognition; we do it because we want to find the answers. Personally, I like to give the victims a voice. In most cases, they didn't deserve to die. They were helpless victims and deserve to have their killers brought to justice.

We spend the next hour filling out the final paperwork, I finally get a chance to write my sexy biker back.

Me: **We fly out in a few hours. Thank God.**

He doesn't respond right away, and it gives me time to finish up the report I'm writing. I hand it over to Dixon before I pack my shit up and make my way out of the police station. I need some fresh air. My mind is swimming, and part of me just thinks that it's because I want to go home. The other part is because I'm dying to get home so I can see Elijah.

Damn, he even has a sexy as fuck name. God, I'm so screwed. As I lean up against the building, my phone starts to buzz in my pocket. When I pull it out, I see his name on the screen. My Sexy Biker.

"Hey," I answer after a few rings.

"Hey back at ya. I got your message. Sorry, I didn't write you back, I've been on a ride." My mind instantly goes to thoughts of him on his bike. I think about the tight muscles in his arms and thighs as he straddles his bike. I feel my dick harden just at the thought of him.

"Spencer." He growls into the phone. I swallow and then finally choke out some words.

"Sorry, I was just thinking about what you'd look like on that bike of yours," I say quietly. I look around me and don't see anyone around.

I hear his chuckle come over the line, it shoots straight to my dick. Fuck, I need him to fuck me already. Getting home is the only thing really on my mind. "When you get home, I want you to meet me at the bar. Same place we met." He murmurs into the other line.

"I'll be there. Same place, same time."

"Good." His voice drops to a husky rasp, I'm about ready to tell my team to get the fuck on the plane so we can get the fuck out of here and back home.

"I'll see you soon." My voice drops and I can feel my heart start to race at the possibilities of tonight. Fuck, I can't wait to see him again.

He doesn't say goodbye as he ends the call. The warm sun feels like it's burning through me as I stare off towards the road. My mind thinks back to the way his hands felt as they ran over my body. The way his mouth felt as it brushed over my skin. My dick hardens, and I can feel how damn tight my pants are getting with just the thought of him touching me.

A hand lands on my shoulder, instantly breaking me from my thoughts of Elijah. When I turn, I see Dixon and the rest of the guys standing close by. "We ready to head out?" I ask. I'm sure that Canaan is going to say something, but I'm surprised when he doesn't. Instead, he just grins and turns to walk towards the SUV's.

By the time we finally get back to the office, I'm fucking

exhausted and ready to get the hell out of there. I glance at my watch and see that it's almost nine p.m., which means I only have about two hours to get to the bar.

As I'm walking towards my desk, Canaan stops me. "I know you don't want to be filling out paperwork all night so head home. You probably got a date lined up already with that biker."

I roll my eyes at him, but he doesn't let me continue to my desk. One thing everyone knows about me is I pull my own weight. I don't like people thinking that I get away with doing less because of my sexual orientation. I got here by my work ethic and smarts. I worked hard to get here, I don't want one date to ruin that.

"Trust me, I got it. You deserve this. I know you want it too." he states. "I'll get you to help me with some paperwork when I'm the one in your shoes." He winks and pushes me towards the door.

"Seriously Canaan, I can do the paperwork and still get there in time," I say frustrated.

"Get the fuck out of here, I got it." He says, pushing me towards the door again. "If you don't leave, I'm leaving instead, and you'll be here all night doing this shit yourself."

Dick. As much as I don't want to leave him to fill out the paperwork alone, I take him up on his offer. If I do paperwork tonight, there is no way I'm going to be getting to the bar in time to meet Elijah. And this is something that I don't want to miss.

CHAPTER NINE

Elijah

By the time I pull my bike into the bar parking lot, I'm already late as fuck. I tried to leave an hour ago, but my damn brother went and fucked shit up for me. I shut off the engine and put my kickstand down quickly. Just as I'm about to get off my bike, I hear a few drunken guys come stumbling out of the bar.

As I make my way towards the door, one of them tries to grab onto me, but I move before he can touch me. I'm on a fucking mission to get to Spencer. The minute I pull open the club door, the loud bass takes over everything. The pounding of the music is nothing new to me. I grew up around the MC, when they had parties, the music was typically loud.

I scan the room quickly, I don't see him anywhere. Just as I'm about to make my way to the bar to find out if the bartender from the other night remembers seeing him here tonight, I spot him. He's got a drink in his hand while swaying to the music.

Instead of walking right over to him, I stand right where I am and just watch him. I'm so entranced by him that I don't notice anything else. He sways his hips to the beat of the song and raises a hand up over his head. He dances as if no one is watching him. What I wouldn't give to be as carefree as he is right

now.

I watch as another guy comes up behind him, but as soon as his hands go to Spencer's hips, he opens his eyes and turns to look at him. He says something before he turns around and goes back to dancing alone. The guy he just dismissed looks pissed and ready to say something to Spencer. Instead of standing back any longer, I make my way over to him.

Just as the fucker is about to put his hand on Spencer again, I grab his wrist and twist is behind his back. When his eyes meet mine, I can see the fear in them. "Stay the fuck away from what's mine," I growl when I lean into his ear.

His eyes widen, and he starts to pull away from me. I don't let others fuck with what's mine. I'm a protective asshole when I need to be. I've spent years learning from my brothers and old man. They taught me to fight for what I want, even if I'm the only one fighting.

I put my hands on his hips, and I pull him into my body. Instead of turning to face me like he did to the other guy, his body melts into mine. "I didn't think you'd show." He murmurs into my ear, just above the music.

"I would have been here on time if my brother didn't fuck something up," I growl. I'm still fucking pissed that I got dragged into his shit.

He grinds his ass back into my dick, I have to close my eyes to get control before I open them again. What I would give to just bend him over something and fuck him hard from behind. I want to take out all my anger and aggression on his beautiful ass, but I can't. I won't use him as my fuck toy. Just spending the short amount of time talking to him since he's been gone has made me crave him, something that has never happened before.

"I thought you were standing me up." His voice has a tinge of sadness in it, and I hate that I was the reason for it. "But now you're here. I want to make the best of it." He turns to face me and wraps his arms around my neck. His mouth parts slightly as he leans in closer, I want nothing more than to take him right here, right now.

He's fucking beautiful; I'm the lucky son of a bitch that gets to call him mine for at least tonight.

I lean in closer, and I can feel his breath fan out across my lips. I lick my lips and let my tongue slowly run over my lips, barely brushing his as I go. "I'll make it up to you."

His hands tangle in the hair at the nape of my neck, and he pulls my head the rest of the distance. The minute our mouths touch, it's like fireworks are exploding. The feel of his mouth on mine is something I didn't even know I was missing until now. My hands slide down his back and grip his ass, pulling him into me. I can feel his dick as he rubs against me. Fuck.

"As much as I want to treat you right, I want to fuck you even more." I groan as he bites my bottom lip with his teeth. The slight tug sends a damn line straight to my dick, I want nothing more than to get the fuck out of here and now.

"Let's get out of here," I whisper into his ear, biting his earlobe. His moan fills my ear, and I make the decision for us. There is no way I'm going to be able to hang on much longer. I can only think about one thing, and right now I'm looking right at it.

Grabbing his hand, I lead him through the crowded bar and towards the exit. A few people try to stop us to talk to him, but I don't allow it. I can't fucking wait any longer. I've been jacking off to the memories of watching him jack off in his hotel room. I need to feel him around me right now.

"You drive this time?" I growl when I bring us to a stop at

my bike.

He leans into me and runs a finger down my week old beard. "No, I took a cab. I was hoping to bum a ride from a hot biker."

"I'll give you more than just one ride." I wink at him and throw my leg over the bike. I wait for him to get on behind me, and the moment he does, I feel the warmth of his body pressing against mine. His thighs squeeze against my hips, and all thoughts go straight to my dick. There is nothing that I can do right now to get rid of the raging hard on I'm currently sporting, instead of even trying, I start the engine and take off into the night.

I pull up to his house, and I park my bike in front of his truck just like I did the last time I was here. Waiting for him to get off, I shut the engine off and rub my hand up and down my still hard dick. Riding in this fucking condition is shitty as fuck, but knowing what was waiting for me when we got here made the trip worth the damn pain.

I watch the way he swings his leg over the side of the bike, and I have to bite my cheek to keep from reaching out to touch him. If I want to get him inside, then I need to be patient.

As he stands there watching me, I feel my heart start to pound. I'm sure I'm going to sound like a pussy, but the way the moonlight is hitting his face right now is almost angelic. Fuck. I'm starting to sound like River.

As I get off my bike, I take a few steps towards him. I don't even have to close the distance between us because he already is. His hand snakes around my back, and he pulls his body to mine. "I've been dying to see you since I left," he rasps. His warm breath tickles along my neck.

"Glad I'm not the only one," I reply, running my hand up his back, stopping it on the back of his neck. My fingers press into his skin, and I pull his mouth to mine. The kiss starts out soft, but turns hungry quickly. My other hand grips his ass and gives it a squeeze. My weakness is a nice ass, and he definitely has one of those.

His tight jeans don't leave much to the imagination. I run my hand up his ass and then slide it into the back of his jeans. He's fucking commando. I groan into his mouth. Fuck I want him so damn bad right now. Instead of necking out in the driveway, I start to walk him backward towards his front door.

When I push him up against the door, he bites down on my bottom lip and sucks it into his mouth. His hands run down my chest and then sneak under my shirt. One of his hands seeks out a nipple, and he pinches it between his thumb and forefinger. "If you don't open the door now, I'm going to fuck you out here for all your neighbors to see."

He bites his lip and then smirks. "They might like the show." I pull my hand out of his jeans and spin him around so that he can face the door. He goes to grab his keys as I undo the button on his jeans. I slide my hand inside quickly and grip his dick. He's hard and waiting just like me. I start to stroke him inside his jeans as he fumbles with the lock.

"You're hard for me." I murmur in his ear. He moans out his answer as he continues to try and unlock the door. "I can't wait to fuck that little asshole of yours." I suck on his neck, and he presses his ass back into me.

The minute the lock on the door clicks, he pushes it open, and I walk with him inside. Kicking the door closed, I push him up against the wall and claim his mouth in a rough, bruising manner. He gives it back just as good as he takes it. His hands grip the bottom of my tee, pulling it up and over my head. He tosses it behind me on the ground and starts to kiss his way down my

chest.

His hands go to my jeans, and he unbuttons them quickly, sliding them down my thighs. My dick springs out of its confines and is right in front of his face. He licks his lips before he wraps them around the head of my dick. I've imagined his mouth wrapped around me again like this since we first met.

He runs his tongue along the head of my dick a few times before he slowly takes me further into his mouth. My hands go to the back of his head, and I slowly start to thrust my hips. He lets me set the pace I want, not complaining when I force him to take too much. His nails dig into my thighs as I continue to slowly thrust in and out of his soft, wet mouth.

"Fuck, your mouth feels so damn good." I groan out. His eyes meet mine, I love the way he keeps eye contact with me. His moans fill the entryway of his house.

Leaning over him, I run my hand down his back and slide them back into his jeans. I run my finger over his puckered hole, causing him to take his mouth off me. I give him a light smack for taking his mouth off me. "Suck me off," I growl. He does just as I say. He takes me back into his mouth and starts to work me up quicker than before.

My hands grab the hem of his shirt on the way up, and I tug it off of him, severing our connection.

CHAPTER TEN

Looking up at the powerful body of Elijah I feel my mouth go dry. There are so many things I want to do to him right now. The taste of him drives me fucking wild, I want more. Fuck, do I want more from him.

"Take me into your mouth," he demands. I look up at him from my position on the floor and slowly move closer to him to take him back into my mouth. I fist the base of his cock and slowly move my hand up and down him as I swirl my tongue along his pierced tip.

His hands bury themselves into my hair, and he gives it a good yank, pulling my head off of him. His eyes follow my tongue as I lick my lips. One of his hands comes down to run gently along my jaw. He leans forward and presses his mouth down to mine. His tongue begs for entrance, I give him what he wants.

As our tongues battle for dominance, his grip on me tightens, and he pulls me up with him. He releases his grip on me and pulls his mouth off of mine. Both of us are panting, I'm hard as fuck. I want to feel him inside of me. I reach out and run my hands down his chest towards his dick. When I reach it, he closes his

eyes and leans his head back. I kneel down at his feet and slightly put my mouth back on his dick, pulling a low moan from his mouth.

I grab his jeans and work them the rest of the way down his strong legs. When they pool at his feet, he steps out of them and gently kicks them off with his boots. Before I can take him into my mouth again, he pulls me up and grabs me around the waist. "Bed." His voice is a harsh whisper against my neck. He bites down on my neck then soothes it with his tongue. I lose all train of thought and forget to actually move. "Now." He growls when we don't move.

I start to move, taking him towards the master bedroom. Before we even get there, he's got his hand going into the back of my jeans. His fingers slip between my ass cheeks, he starts to run his finger up and down. I grab the door knob to my room and manage to get it open. He pushes the door open behind me. Walking me backward towards the bed, he pushes me back onto it.

I watch the way his eyes are eating me up right now, and it's a huge turn on. His eyes are scanning down my body and then back up to my face. Every step he takes towards me kicks my heartbeat up. His hands go to the back of my neck, and he pulls my face to his. He gently kisses me before letting his hands roam down my body, and straight to the jeans I'm still wearing.

With the flick of his wrist, he undoes the button and pulls the zipper down. Breaking the kiss, he pushes me back on the bed, and I go willingly. Putting my feet on the bed frame, I lift my hips up to help him pull my jeans past my ass and towards my feet. He pulls them off of me along with my black converses I was wearing.

Slowly he kisses his way up my body until he comes to my cock. He runs his tongue along the underside of my cock until he grips it and runs his tongue along the head. The minute he takes me into his mouth completely, I forget how to breathe. My hand grips his brown hair, and my fingers tangle in the longer strands. His mouth bobs up and down on my shaft. He takes me to the back of his throat, every moan he makes brings me closer to the edge. When his eyes meet mine, I'm done for. He's fucking beautiful in a rough sort of way. What most people probably see as a rough on the outside biker, I see the man that is hidden under the tattoos and the leather jacket he wears.

When he pulls his mouth off of me, he kisses his way up my body until he comes to my mouth. He fucks my mouth with his. His tongue glides along my teeth before he starts to pull away, biting my bottom lip and sucking it between his teeth.

"I want to fuck you so badly right now." He growls when he releases my lip.

"Then fuck me," I say on a gasp. His hand grips my dick, and he slowly strokes me. He kisses me slowly before he pushes himself up and off the bed.

He flips me over onto my stomach. When I look behind me, I see him sink to his knees. His hands spread my ass cheeks, and he slowly runs his tongue along my hole. When his mouth leaves my hole, his finger takes its place. He slowly starts to press his finger inside of me.

My whole body tenses as he starts to press inside of me, I can't help it. It's been a while since I've been with someone. "I'm not going to hurt you." His rasp eases my tension, I can hear how much he wants me in his words. "Fuck, you've got a body for sin." His other hand trails up my back and his fingers gently trail over my skin, leaving goosebumps in their path. "I can't wait to know what you feel like wrapped around my dick."

My breath catches at his words. "Do you have lube?" I nod

my head, unable to get the words out of my mouth. "Drawer?" he asks. I nod again, and his body heat leaves mine as he walks over to my dresser that is next to the bed. He opens the first one and slowly looks through it. He grabs it and starts to stalk back towards me. I hear him pop the cap on the bottle before he snaps it closed and tosses it on the bed next to me.

The cold liquid hits my skin, he slowly starts to massage it into my asshole. He first sinks one finger in, working it inside of me. My moans start to fill the room, soon he's pushing another finger inside of me. He starts to scissor his fingers in and out of me. With every stroke of his finger, I can feel him opening me up wider. "Fuck, you feel so damn good on my fingers." He groans into my ear.

He continues to stretch me, adding a finger here and there. I start to stroke my cock, I swear I could come at any moment. It feels that damn good. When he thrusts his finger in and to the left, I can't help but moan out loudly when he hits my prostate. Fuck that feels amazing. His fingers hit it again causing my body to jerk on the bed. "Oh God." I whimper out. The feeling is out of this world. I don't think I've ever had someone do that to me before.

I've heard about it before, but never experienced it. Not like this. Fuck. "Please fuck me, Eli." I breathe out as he slams his fingers back inside of me.

"Best fucking words I've ever heard all fucking week." He releases me, and I feel the cold air as it hits my naked body. I hear the sound of his feet padding against my hardwood floors. The sound of my drawer opening again fills the room along with my ragged breathing. Holy fuck. I can't wait to feel that big cock of his filling me. His footsteps are coming back towards me, I hear the distinct sound of the condom wrapper as he rips it open. I watch him slide it down his length and then reach out to grab the lube.

He squeezes a generous amount on his dick and then

starts to run his hand up and down his shaft. When he makes his way back towards me, I can feel my heart hammering in my chest. "I love seeing your ass out just like this. You like to be spanked?" His eyebrow rises with his question, I forget to speak. I swear you would think that I was a mute or something when I'm around him.

"I asked if you liked being spanked." As soon as the words are out of his mouth, his hand comes down on my ass cheek. I can't help the small yelp that comes from my mouth.

"Yeah Eli, I do. But I want you to fuck me. Please?" I beg. Fuck, he has no idea how much I want him inside of me right now. I want it more than my next breath.

I hear him chuckle before I feel his body heat getting closer to me. His hands slide down my back and stop on my ass cheeks. He gives each cheek a squeeze before he opens me wide and rubs the head of his dick into my opening. "I can't wait to sink inside of you." His husky voice only turns me on more.

"Then fuck me." I bite out. I'm tired of his teasing. I want him in me now. I reach behind me and grab his hip, pulling him into me. The head of his dick slowly starts to slide inside of me, I feel the familiar stretch.

Once he gets past my ring of muscle, we both groan together. His chest is now resting on my back as he takes a few deep breaths, calming himself. "Fuck," he mutters.

"Move Eli. I need you to move." I whimper. His teeth graze my ear, I feel his warm breath spread over me.

"If I move now, I'm going to come." His harsh whisper tells me that he's barely holding on. "You're so fucking tight." I can feel his heart racing as he lies on top of me. I feel his breathing slow down and finally he starts to move. Slow, deep thrusts. Each plunge hits right when I want it, I can feel the jolt in my body as he hits my prostate. I moan into the bedspread.

78

"Harder," I grunt out as his hand comes down on my ass cheek. Each move of his hips brings me closer to the edge and fuck does it feel amazing. No other man has ever made me feel the way he does. His hand grips my length, and he starts to slide his hand up and down it with long, hard strokes in time with his dick.

"Oh God," I whine. I'm about to fucking come. There is nothing that is going to stop it right now. It feels way too damn good. "Christ, I'm going to come." He picks up his pace and fucks me harder. The slapping of his thighs hitting the back of mine and our grunts are the only sounds in the room.

"Come for me." He demands in my ear. His lips trail along my neck, and they hover over my pulse. The minute his teeth sink into my skin, I come.

"Fuck, fuck, fuck!" I yell out as I grip the blankets. His hand continues to stroke me I as come all over the side of the bed and blankets. As I'm coming down from my orgasm, I feel him pull away from me. Before I can even make sense of anything again, I feel his warm cum hitting my bare skin. His grunts fill my room and I just close my eyes, reveling in the amazing way he's made me feel tonight.

His lips land in the middle of my back and he kisses his way up to my neck. "That was fucking amazing." He says in between kisses. His finger runs up and down my back and starts to rub small circles in certain places.

When I look over my shoulder at him, he's rubbing his semen into my skin, marking me in a way.

CHAPTER ELEVEN

Elijah

After the amazing sex, I dragged his sexy as fuck ass up to the pillows and cuddled in behind him. My hand is resting on his throat, and his ass is pressed firmly into my dick. The feel of his body against mine is like heaven, and if I had the choice, I'd never leave.

"You going to stay?" he mumbles. His breathing is evening out, I know he's about to pass out. I weight my options. I have church first thing to go over the shit my brothers found out about the dead bitch on our turf.

"Yeah," I whisper against the side of his neck and bury my face into it. It's been a long time since I've stayed after sex. I'm not the type to want to cuddle and talk afterward. I like to get off and then get the fuck out.

My eyes close and I start to drift off to sleep with this good-looking man when my phone starts to ring out in the other room. The loud ringtone isn't one I recognize right off the bat, so I extract myself from him and make my way towards the sound. When I finally get to it, I see that I have eight missed calls from my brothers.

Rubbing my hands down my face, I try to figure out what the fuck they'd be calling about at this fucking hour. When I put the phone to my ear and start to listen to the voicemails, I know this shit is just getting worse. With all the shit that went down a few months ago, I can't help but think about Raef when I see all the missed calls. Raef may not have been my brother by blood, but he was my brother. We grew up together. The six of us boys were pretty much inseparable as we were growing up. Although we didn't have much choice, we didn't care. We all clicked.

Ever since his death, we've been pulled together even tighter than before. When shit goes down, we call each other. I think part of it may be because we were there to witness it. We watched as the bullet tore right through his chest. Just thinking about it brings back the bad memories. I have to fight back the tears at the thought of Sailor screaming as she watched him take the bullet that was meant for his old man.

The only shitty thing is that she's pulled away from us. She refuses to talk to anyone but Prez and Anslie. Even then I hear that it's hard to get her to talk to them. I'm sure she blames us for his death and hell, I'm sure if I was in her situation, I would too. But he died protecting his family. Something he swore to do.

We all wanted to follow in our father's footsteps. Even I did. Being as different as I am than the others, I still respect the hell out of my old man and our Prez.

Hitting the call button on Brant's name, I wait for him to answer. When our old man steps down, he's the next in line. I can't imagine the stress he feels about that shit. He's always been the one to keep us walking the straight and narrow even when he was fucking up. Personally, I think he'll be a great vice president. He's always had a way of getting people to follow him just like Dominic.

"About fucking time asshole." He grunts into the phone.

"I've been a little busy." I grit out. I don't question them when they don't answer.

"I don't care if you're fucking the damn queen, answer your damn phone." I hear him say something to someone, but his words are too mumbled to hear them clearly. "We were going to call church tonight, but a few of the brothers weren't answering. It's scheduled for eight a.m. Don't be fucking late or dad will have your ass." I roll my eyes. Dad doesn't say shit when we're late. Plus, I've never been late to church before; I'm not going to start now.

"What the fuck is the big deal?" I ask. I'm fucking tired, and all I want to do is climb back into bed with Spencer.

"Prez got some news about how that bitch that took Axle ended up on our steps." This peaks my interest. I've been trying to figure that shit out since we found her.

"Why?"

I hear him sigh and I'm sure he's rubbing his hand across his beard. "Hold on, let me go to my office. I don't want Anslie to hear this shit." His voice is a soft whisper. Shit, it might be worse than I thought.

I hear the click of a door over the phone and what sounds like his feet hitting the top of his desk. "So you remember Anslie's mom right?"

"Yeah, the crazy bitch that took her from Prez," I state. I remember we were little tots when that shit went down, but we heard all about it as we got older.

"Well when shit went down with Ryder and his ole' lady, she was at the strip club. I guess she's been hanging around town. Prez is fucking pissed and so am I. I'm not letting that bitch come anywhere near my girl or my kids." He blows out a harsh

breath over the line.

"What does this have to do with the bitch who kidnapped Dom's kid?" I still don't see the connection.

"The tape caught sight of her just outside of the gates. You don't notice her because you're not looking, but it's fucking her. It almost looks like Ans on the tape." I think back to the tape and try to remember if I saw her or not.

"I thought it was two men who dropped the bitch off?" I ask.

"It was. But I think she came with them or was trying to get some dirt. Shit, I don't know. I forced Anslie to tell me what her bitch of a mom was texting her. I still can't believe they've kept me in the fucking dark." I snort at that. Does he really mean that shit? Hell, even I can see why they did it. He's a damn loose cannon when it comes to her, especially since she's going to give birth at any moment.

"Trust me, it was a good idea that they did. You would have gone in guns blazing and who the fuck knows what would have happened." He chuckles but doesn't disagree. He could have gotten himself killed and then where would she and the kids be.

"I think her mom has something to do with this shit. Raef's death, her showing up, and that bitch being dumped at the clubhouse." He continues talking, but I hear Spencer's footsteps.

"Hey, I have to go. I'll see you in the morning."

"You with some bitch?" he asks.

"I'll see you tomorrow," I say again. He grumbles something into the phone, but I don't catch the words because I'm too busy watching the way Spencer is walking towards me. His eyes never leave my face as I tell my oldest brother bye and hang up before he can continue talking.

"Everything okay?" His sleepy voice is sexy as fuck.

"Yeah, it was my brother. I was just coming back to bed." His arm wraps around my waist, and he pulls me to him.

"Good. The bed was really lonely without you." He gives me a shy, sleepy smile. I start to walk him backward, and I lean down to kiss his lips. "How many brothers do you have?" his question is quite cute in his sleepy state.

"I have three by blood." He raises an eyebrow at me and waits for me to expand on that further. "Biker brothers babe." He nods slightly.

When we come to the bedroom, I spin him around and force him to walk to the bed. Once he climbs in, I get in right beside him. He turns to face me, and I get this sudden urge to kiss him. Every time I look into his eyes, I see a part of me that I never knew I was looking for. It's almost like he accepts me. I know it sounds fucking crazy, especially since we've known each other less than a week.

Something in his eyes calls to me, dragging me out of the fucking hell I feel like I've been trapped in all my life.

"Why are you staring at me like that?" he asks with a smile.

"I don't know. I guess because when I look at you, I don't see the judgment." His smile turns into a frown, and he reaches up to run his fingers down the side of my face, brushing some of my hair out of my eyes.

"Why would I judge you? We're more alike than you probably realize." I stare at him for a few minutes before I say anything.

"We are nothing alike. I'm probably the worse man for you to be with." I watch his eyebrows scrunch together, and when he goes to say something, I stop him. Putting my finger to his lips, I silence his words. "Trust me; I'm not a good guy. I don't deserve the happily ever after, and I know that I'll screw this up in a day or two."

"You have no idea what you're talking about." he murmurs. His mouth presses against mine in a sweet kiss that rocks me to my core. He thinks he knows me, but he doesn't. Sure we texted back and forth a little while he was gone, but I didn't even skim the surface. I told him I was a biker, but he has no idea that I'm part of the Wayward Saints. We've been deemed some of the worse men in Las Vegas, even though people don't really know us.

We are just like every other club out there, but we are focused on our family. Have we killed? Yeah, we do what we have to. After Raef's death, we've been trying like hell to take the bastards down. A few of them got away, and I wish like hell we could track them, but we can't. We've hit every damn road block possible.

"You're better than me," I mumble against his lips.

"I don't think so." He responds, pulling me closer to his body. His face buries itself into my neck, and I feel his warm breath fans across it. Just having him in my arms right now makes it seem like I can have the good life my brothers have. That I can fall for someone and not be judged.

Who am I kidding? As soon as my brothers find out, it's going to be fucking hell. I know my mom thinks that my brothers are going to accept me with open arms, but I'm skeptical. They are set in their own thoughts, and there isn't a damn thing I'll be able to do to change their minds. I've heard the stories from the old days. I've heard what they've done to men who came out as gay in the MC world.

It's not an easy road, even though I'm terrified of stumbling down the road, I think that Spencer would be worth the trouble. The attraction I feel for him is undeniable. There is no way that I'll be able to walk away from him after tonight. He's already burying himself into me inch by inch, I'm just as excited as I am scared of it.

He will be my downfall. Protecting him from my brothers is something I'll do if the situation arises.

CHAPTER TWELVE

Spencer

Waking up wrapped in his arms is probably hands down the best way to wake up. His strong arms tighten around me and pull me closer to his body. I melt into his embrace and close my eyes. Before I can fall back asleep, my phone starts to ring in my pants pocket. Groaning, I rub my hand over my eyes and then start to pull away from his body. After a kiss to the back of my neck, he releases me and lets me get up.

Stalking over to my jeans from last night, I find my phone and see Dixon's name on the screen. Hitting the answer button, I put it to my ear and breathe a hello.

"Sorry to call so early. I just got a new case on my desk, and it's a hot one. I need you here ASAP."

"Got it. I'm going to shower first." I grumble. I had some dirty plans that I was hoping to take advantage of while I had Elijah in my bed. When I look over at the bed, I see him leaning up on his elbow, watching every move I make. Dixon says something else, but I completely miss it. The line goes dead, and I just continue to stare at the sexy biker that is currently taking up his fair share of my bed.

"Don't worry about it. I need to go anyway. I have to meet my brothers in an hour." I take a deep breath and walk over towards him.

"I just hate that I keep getting called away." When I get close enough, he wraps his arm around me and pulls me closer to him. I fall onto the bed and land on his chiseled chest.

"Don't." He presses his mouth to mine, and I let my mind go blank. I don't think about anything but the two of us. His hand slides up to cup my neck as he kisses me without any shame. His tongue slips into my mouth, and I massage his with mine.

My hands go to his chest and just as I'm about to crawl back into bed with him for a few more minutes, his phone starts to ring. Closing my eyes, I sigh and pull away from him. "Sorry," he groans. When he looks at his screen, he rolls his eyes and hits the answer button before saying, "What?" to whoever is on the other side of the phone.

"Oh hey, little man." He pauses for a second before he says something else. "No, I'll talk to your daddy about it. Me, you, and Sev can go to the movies without that lame daddy of yours." He grins, and when he looks up at me, I see happiness that I've only seen once before. "Yeah, we can do a man's day. No mom allowed." He chuckles at whatever response he gets and then asks to talk to the little one's dad.

"Yeah, I'm heading that way in a few." He looks over at me before he smirks again. "Naw, I'm an hour out." He sits up and presses his mouth silently to mine. "No, I'm not bringing River." He says as he pulls his mouth from mine. Instead of getting in between him and whoever he's talking to, I make my way towards my closet to pull on some clothes. I'm already running late, and if I shower, there is no way I'll make it in time for the case briefing.

I can hear parts and pieces of his conversation, but I hate

eavesdropping. Instead, I focus on getting ready and repacking my go bag for my truck. Hopefully, I won't have to use it again so soon, but it wouldn't be the first time. With the rate the cases have been going lately, we've spent more time in other states than our own.

Once I set my bag by the bedroom door, I feel hands on my hips. He moves his hands up my chest and presses his lips against my neck. "You going out of town again?"

I try to turn to face him, but he doesn't let me go. "Don't know until after I get to the office." I murmur, giving him better access to my neck. He sucks and nips along my neck and then back down to my collarbone before he finally pulls away.

"If you stay local, let me know. I'd love to see you again." His lips make me forget everything I was just thinking about. My breathing hitches as he runs his tongue along my neck. Reaching behind me, I feel that he's now got his jeans back on, but is still missing his shirt. He must have brought them in here last night when he went to answer his phone.

"As soon as I know, I'll send you a text." He nips at my earlobe in answer, I can't help the groan that falls from my lips. Fuck, I love the way his mouth feels on me.

"You better. I'm nowhere near done with you." My dick hardens at his words. Fuck, I wish I could go back to bed with him right now instead of work. He releases me with one more kiss on my neck. When I turn to look at him, I feel like the wind gets knocked out of me.

His hooded eyes bring me in, and I want to get lost in them. He's everything I've always wanted and never knew I'd find, wrapped up in a bad boy biker package. Someone in my field should stay the fuck away from him. If my superiors found out, I could lose my job. Hell, I could lose everything I've worked so damn hard for.

I don't know a whole lot about his biker life, but I can only hope that they are a riding club and not one of the MC's that the local cops have been trying to shut down for years.

By the time I get to the office, I'm already fifteen minutes late. I spent a little longer wrapped up in his arms than I should have, but I don't regret a minute of it. Besides my job, getting to talk to him has been the highlights of my days. I know I shouldn't think that way, but it's hard not to. It's like I just know. I just know that he is the one I was meant to find. Kind of like that fairytale romance that women believe in. The romance that makes it seem like for the first time, everything is in color and not just black and white anymore.

As soon as I drop my go bag on the floor next to my desk, and set my computer down on my chair, Dixon is calling us all into the conference room. I make my way towards the conference room and see the rest of the guys following behind me. As I take a seat in the chair closest to my right, I see Milli standing off to the side looking a little hesitant.

The reason she only looks hesitant is if the crime is a really violent one or children. I just pray that we aren't going on another child abduction case. Those ones are the ones that hit me the worse. My little brother was a victim of a child abduction case when we were younger. It's part of the reason I wanted to be in this unit. I wanted to be able to track down the sick sons of bitches that think hurting children is okay.

There isn't a day that I don't think about his disappearance or the way it destroyed our family. My parents never spoke to each other after that day. I watched their once loving and happy marriage fizzle out like the remnants of the fire my dad set to burn every memory of their once happy life.

My mom became unfit to raise me, and I was left to be in the care of my father. He became a cold bastard after Talon died. He couldn't even look at me without seeing my little brothers face. He resented the fact that I was still alive and my little brother wasn't. He told me I didn't protect him the way I should have.

I knew he was angry, but as a kid it destroyed me. As I got older, I made it my mission to stay out of his way. I only came out of my room when it was necessary and never when he was drinking.

A hand on my shoulder brings me away from my memories. "You alright?" Fox whispers. I nod my head and look up to the front where I see the photos from the new case. Fuck. The scenes in front of me make my stomach turn.

How the fuck are people okay with this shit?

My eyes lock on the first photo. Now I can see why Milli had that look on her face. My eyes scan over every inch of the photo. The woman looks like someone bashed her head in with something. She's almost unrecognizable. Her blonde hair is matted to her head with dark blood. I scan down her body and see the marks covering most of her skin. Welts, burns, and cuts cover most of her arms and bare stomach.

Whoever fucking did this is a God damn animal. Her clothes are practically torn off of her, and most of the cuts look deep. She probably passed out from the pain that this bastard was inflicting on her.

"This woman is believed to be part of a sex trafficking ring. The man was in charge of it is at large, and we believe that a few of the local motorcycle clubs are helping get the girls to them. There are a few other players that include a drug cartel and a few others that we have no information on yet."

"Fuck," I mutter. I look at the next photo and see another blonde who looks like someone beat the fuck out of her. She is covered in bruises, and when my eyes get to her naked skin, I see a brand on her skin. When I suck in a breath, all the eyes shoot towards me. I've seen the brand before. I can feel my breathing start to quicken, and the spots swim in my vision.

There is no fucking way. No God damn way.

Getting up out of my chair, I dash towards the bathroom. The urge to throw up is way stronger than I am. Pushing open one of the stalls, I dry heave into the toilet. I hear the door to the bathroom open, but I ignore Canaan as he says my name.

"Spence, you good?" he asks.

I wipe my mouth and spit into the toilet a few times before I flush it. When I come out of the stall, Canaan is standing by the sinks, leaning against the wall. He doesn't say anything when I walk over towards him to wash out my mouth with the water from the tap. Instead, he hands me a paper towel and waits silently.

"I'm fine." My tone comes off bitchier than I intended. The sight of that brand brings back the memories I've tried like hell to forget.

"You don't look fine," he mutters. Just as I turn to face him, he continues. "What the fuck was that? I've known you awhile now, and nothing phases you when it comes to cases. You're always the one to see between the damn lines and get us into the right direction. What the fuck made you dash into the bathroom to throw up?"

I don't bother answering him. Instead, I take off towards my desk and grab my phone out of my bag, with Canaan right on my heels. "Seriously Spence, what the fuck is going on?"

I spin around and put my finger into his chest. "Stay the

fuck out of it." A clearing of a throat brings my attention to the rest of the guys and Milli. All eyes are on me, I can feel the anger start to bring itself to the surface. There is no fucking way I'm talking about this shit. No damn way.

CHAPTER THIRTEEN

Elijah

As soon as I pull into the clubhouse parking lot, I see the brothers all gathered around by the bike shop. After parking and getting off my bike, I make my way towards the crowd. Putting my hand on Brantley's shoulder, I see all the long faces. "What's going on?" I whisper to him.

He looks at me and then nods towards our old man. "Our old man got a visit from some Fed." I feel my eyebrows shoot up as I stare at our father.

"For what?" I ask. A few of the guys turn to look at me, but I ignore them.

"They think we have something to do with some case their working on. Instead of letting them go after Prez, he stepped up and took the questioning." I frown and look back at our father. He's pissed, and he and Prez seem to be in a heated discussion that no one but them can hear. The door to the office is shut, and no one is allowed in. All of us are pretty much gathered around the office door like bitches waiting to hear the latest gossip.

As soon as they stop their yelling match, they turn to look at us all gathered outside. When the door opens, I can see the

anger radiating off our old man. He's pissed, and I don't get why.

"Church!" Prez yells from behind our old man. The guys start to make their way towards church, I follow behind Brant and Jase.

"What do you think it's about?" I ask.

It's Jase who answers me this time. "I'm thinking the body yesterday." Before I can say anything, he changes the subject. "Where the fuck were you last night? We called for a straight fucking hour!" I shrug off his question, but he doesn't let it go all that easy.

"You fucking some chick you don't want the rest of us to know about? Does that mean you and River are over?" I swear sometimes it's like a damn soap opera with these dick heads.

"I don't know how many times I have to say that River and I aren't together. Never have been, never will be. She's in love with that bastard Seb. Go bust his balls for not making a move on her." They both start to laugh, I know they aren't going to do shit. Because just like everyone else, they think that River and I are together.

By the time we are all gathered in church and in our seats, Prez is slamming the gavel down on the table. The loud crack of it hitting the table echoes through the room and everyone becomes silent.

My old man puts his hands together in a prayer-like symbol, and both of his pointer fingers are pressed to his lips, almost like he's trying to keep himself from saying something.

"Shit's about to get a whole lot worse before it gets better for us," Prez says, his voice low and dark. Ever since Raef's death, Prez has been angrier than before. My old man said he hasn't been this bad since Avelyn died.

"We lost a brother, a son. Now the Feds are trying to pin the deaths of women on us. That bitch that kidnapped Axle, she is one of the women they think we killed. Although I wish it was us who ended her, I know we didn't touch her." He runs his fingertips along the table in front of him for a few minutes before he looks up at us. "I want revenge on the fuckers who killed my son. I want to find these fuckers that are trying to take us down. Those bastards wanted Sailor and I sure as shit ain't letting anything happen to her." His eyes scan the table, and when he gets to my old man, he nods his head.

"She's being protected. Sailor is under our protection because it's what Raef wanted. She may be trying to keep us at arm's length, but I'm not letting anything happen to his girl." We all nod our heads to his statement. "Nick and I have been talking about our next move. We are trying to let her live her life in Sacramento as she wants, but we need eyes on her. Sacramento says they've got it. Right now, I'm going to trust them. I got rid of the bastards who didn't believe the shit Raef was saying. I replaced them with men that I trust."

Silence in the room is deafening. I can hear my own heartbeat thumping clearly. The mention of Raef and Sailor bring back all the fucking thoughts of what happened that day. I try to push that shit out of my head, but it all comes pouring back in like it was happening now. I was right by Prez when Raef threw himself in front of that bullet. I should have taken that bullet instead of him. I didn't have a girl I was madly in love with like he did. I wouldn't have let the love of my life watch as I died on the fucking ground.

I close my eyes and try to fight back the memories and all the things I wish I would have done to save him. She needs him more than the brothers need me right now.

A few throats clear around the table, I know that this shit affects us all still. Six months doesn't seem like nearly enough

time when you think about it. It still feels like just yesterday.

"What are we going to do?" I ask. I can't continue to think about Raef and Sailor without fucking breaking down, wishing things were different. I need to focus on something I can do now. I need to know what our options are. Who we are going after? We need to find the fuckers who put the bullet in his damn chest and stop waiting to strike them.

"A source in the department said they think that bastard from the strip club Anslie's mom was hanging around might be involved which means I'm going to pay that bitch a visit."

Brant stands from his seat, and I can see the anger radiating off of him.

"Sit," Prez demands. Brant doesn't move, and I have to give him credit for that. He may be fucking Prez's daughter, but it doesn't mean he can deny an order.

"No. I want to take that bitch down. She's been doing nothing but fucking with my girl's head. I'm sick of her shit, and I'm done watching my girl cry herself to sleep every night." I can feel the change in the damn room at his statement. Judging by the look on Prez's face, he didn't know it had gotten that bad between Anslie and her mom.

"She's been calling?" He growls from the head of the table.

"Yeah. She was still hiding that shit from me because of your order. When I wake up to my pregnant ole' lady crying in the middle of the night, I get a little pissed. I forced her to tell me the truth. She told me she's been getting calls and texts from that bitch since we seen her at the damn club. She saw us. She knew we were there and now she's trying to get back at us for taking Danielle."

I see Ryder tense up in his seat. Ever since he pulled

Danielle out of that strip club, he's been over protective of her. I get why he did that shit too. Her then boyfriend was slapping her around and forcing her to sell herself to the customers. We found out that Anslie's bitch of a mom was back in town for who knows what reason too. "If she comes at Ellie, I won't hesitate to put a bullet in her. She won't fuck with my woman." He's pissed now too. Pretty soon this shit is going to just get worse, and nothing is going to get solved.

"Ryder, I've known you a long time, but you won't kill anyone unless it's sanctioned. We are under a lot of heat, and I won't let any of you get thrown in jail for this shit." My old man says quietly. Prez nods his head in agreement, and Brant takes his seat again.

"We need to get a handle on all those bastards that were left from the shit that went down in Sacramento. I need you guys to put some feelers out. I want answers about who is still standing after we took most of them down. If I need to, I'll talk to Sailor again." Heads start to nod at the words Prez says, and I can feel the tension in the room. Everyone is pissed for different reasons, but mainly it's because we've always been two steps behind those bastards even after that shit went down in Sacramento.

"I don't want you guys out unless you have someone else with you," Prez says more as an afterthought. "I have no idea if someone is going to strike or if the Feds are going to try and haul any of our asses into the station because of this shit. Stay fucking alert. Keep the women and children safe."

He slams the gavel on the table ending church. The crack echoes through the room, I go to stand up. My brother's hand on my shoulder stops me. When I turn to look at Seb, I can't read his expression. It's a mix of anger and something else. "We need to talk." I nod my head and follow him out towards the back of the clubhouse. We walk through the kid's area and up the stairs towards the game room.

When he comes to a stop in front of the pool table, I stop too. "What?" I ask. I already feel on edge with the shit that's been going on. I want the club to go back to the way we were before all the drama and wars started. I liked it better when we were a damn family first and everything else second. We worked, had fun, and celebrated life. We didn't see death. We didn't lose our brothers.

"Why the fuck was River at a club alone last night?" The rage fills his expression. I should have known he would be pissed about her. He's always pissed when it comes to her.

"I've told you time and time again, she's not my girl. She fucks who she wants, when she wants. If she wants to go to a damn club, that's her business, not mine." He puts his hand on my chest and pushes me back.

"She's been your damn girl since high school." he growls.

"River and I have never been together. Everyone just assumes that shit." He stares at me as he takes my words in. "She's been in love with you for years. I've tried to get that shit through your damn head, but you don't fuckin' listen."

"I'm not going after your girl." He sighs, stepping back and leaning against the pool table again.

"You wouldn't be. She's my best friend, and that's it." I state. He frowns and I know he's trying to figure out something in his head.

"Then where the fuck did you disappear to last night?" I shrug. I don't want to answer that. There is no way that he's going to accept that I'm gay. Out of my brothers, I think only Brant will understand. I don't think he'd judge me. He may give me shit for it, but he'd never judge me like the others will.

"I went for a ride." He raises an eyebrow at my answer, but doesn't ask anything else. He lets it go for once. Just as he turns to walk away, I feel my phone vibrate in my pocket.

River: **E, I need you.**

When he sees my face, he stops. She doesn't typically need me. She typically tells me to get my ass to her house now. Hell, she never calls me E either. Something's wrong. I don't even say anything as I push past Sebastian. He follows me through the clubhouse and out towards the bike. I get on my bike and crank the engine, with him doing the exact same thing.

The brothers try to get my attention, but the only thing I can think about is getting to River. She needs me, and I won't let anything happen to her.

CHAPTER FOURTEEN

After my little scene with Canaan, Dixon pulled me into his office. As I'm sitting here staring at the man I've called my boss for the last three years, I can't help but think that I may need to pull away from this case. It's bringing up bad memories that I can't deal with right now.

"What happened in there?" He finally asks after we've been sitting in the silence for the last five minutes.

"I can't work this case," I state. I don't want to get into it, but I know he's not going to give me a choice. We don't get to pick and choose the cases we work. We are a team, and we take every case on together.

"Why?" he demands.

I sit back in my chair and stare at the bookshelf behind him. Trying to find the words is even more difficult than I expected. I try to open my mouth and say the words, but nothing comes out. Instead, he starts to talk. "I've read your file. I know about your little brother's disappearance when you were a child, and I know what happened to your mother. You recognized the brand on one of the victims."

If he knew all this shit then why the fuck is he asking me. I close my eyes and take a deep breath. "Yes," I whisper. I feel like all my defenses are falling around me and there is nothing that I can do to stop them. I don't want to talk about them. I don't want to remember the pain I felt when I had to go and identify my mother because my bastard of a father didn't give two shits about her after my brother died.

Instead, I lost the two of the people I loved the most. Well, three. After my mom's death, my father's drinking got worse, and he was never the same. He was angry all the time, I could see the pain in his eyes the minute he sobered up again.

"I can't go there," I say with as much conviction as I can muster. It sounds weak even to my own ears, but I let him make the final decision.

"You mean you don't want to catch the bastards who did this to her?" His eyes never leave me, and suddenly I feel like I'm standing next to a fire in the middle of the summer. Sweat is starting to dust my hairline, and I can feel the sweat as it starts to drip down my back.

"I just can't. I want that bastard to rot in hell, but I can't see my mother's face every time I look at those photos." My voice trails off towards the end, and I want to get the fuck out of his office. I want to go home and head back to bed. Hell, I would give anything to rewind back to this morning when I had Elijah's strong arms wrapped around me, holding my body to his.

"You're not going to like my answer." I nod my head because I know what he's about to say. "Take the rest of the day off. Come in tomorrow, and we can go from there. We need you on this case. I know you've been looking into it when you get the down time. There might be things that you've noticed along the

way that can help." He doesn't continue, and I'm grateful for it.

Most cops would jump at the thought of being able to find their mother's killer, but I'm not one of them. The road I've traveled since she died is the hardest one I've ever endured. I don't want to go back down the road, but I also want closure. I want to be able to tell my drunk of an old man that I found who killed her. Hell, I want to be able to find out who killed my little brother too.

They say that Jeffery White killed my little brother, but the timeline and evidence never lined up. I've actually visited Jeffery in prison when I was a detective. I got the same answers they got all of those years ago. If he was lying, the story would have varied, but not Jeffery's. His story was exactly the same as the day he was interviewed.

I get out of the chair I'm occupying, and I make my way towards the door. "Thank you," I mumble. He nods his head, and I turn to walk out of his office and towards my desk. I grab my bag and head towards the elevator. I hear my name called, but I don't respond. There is nothing I can say to make this sick feeling go away. Knowing that I am going to be working this case in the morning makes me sick to my damn stomach.

I'm going to find out exactly what she went through before she died. I'm going to picture her face on the new victims, and I'm going to find the person responsible for the crime.

As soon I get to my house, I walk inside and get a whiff of Elijah. The smell of grease and motor oil fill my entry way. The moment I throw myself on my bed, I smell him. A scent that I can only describe as Elijah covers my pillows and my blanket. Grabbing my phone from my pocket, I find his number and type out a text.

Me: *So I have the rest of the day off, you care to come join me?*

He doesn't respond, so I can only imagine what he's doing. Instead of thinking about him with someone else, I pull the covers over my head and shut my eyes. Maybe when I wake up, this will be just a sick dream.

The sound of my phone beeping wakes me. Grabbing the damn thing, I hit the center button and wait for the screen to turn on. When I click the messages, I see Canaan's name on the screen.

Canaan: **Everything good?**

Rubbing my hand over my face, I roll over to my stomach and start to write him back.

Me: **No.**

His response is immediate. Once thing about Canaan that I admire is he's persistent. If he doesn't get an answer to his question, he keeps coming back with the same question until he gets an answer.

Canaan: **Come open the door.**

I groan and roll over to my back. Of course, that bastard is here. He wasn't going to let that shit slide today. I should have known. Getting up from my bed, I stalk through the house and make my way to the front door. As soon as I open it, he's pushing his way inside, and he's got a twelve pack of beer.

I watch him walk towards the kitchen and put the beer in the fridge, keeping two for us. He pops the caps and sets them on the counter before coming back towards me, handing me one. I walk towards the couch and take a seat, leaning my head back against the cushions.

"You want to talk about what happened?" He finally asks after a few beats.

"Not really," I mutter. He doesn't get that this shit lives within me and I rather not dwell on it any more than I have to right now. Tomorrow I'm going to get thrown into this case, and I don't know how I'm going to deal with it.

"We've been friends for a while now. I'm not going to push you into telling me, but just know that I'm here if you need to talk." He kicks his feet up on my coffee table and leans back on the couch.

"Thanks, man," I say quietly. Just as I'm about to say something else to him, my phone buzzes with a new message. I see Elijah's name that he left in my phone and I can't help but grin. Even though it's taken him hours, I'm still glad to see his name on my screen.

My Sexy Biker: *Sorry babe. I've got shit to deal with here and just got your message. If I can break free tonight, I'll stop by.*

I frown, and I can feel Canaan's eyes on me. "Your fuck buddy fall through for tonight?" he jokes.

"He said he has some shit going on." I write out a quick reply and toss my phone on the coffee table. It's not like I'll be getting anymore messages while he's busy doing whatever. Plus the chief won't let anyone at the office call me tonight anyways.

"How did you get the night off?" I ask. I know for sure that Dixon wouldn't let the whole team have the night off if we were on a case.

"We are waiting on some test results and waiting for a few more files to be dropped off. We've interviewed a couple of motorcycle clubs and the victims' families. Not much more we can do tonight." He rolls his shoulders as if he's trying to get a picture off his mind.

"How many victims so far?" I ask.

"Three that we know of." He answers slowly. I can feel the doom floating over my head right now. He's going to say that my mother was one of the victims. By now I'm sure the whole team knows about her. I close my eyes to keep from lashing out at Canaan. It's not his fault. He wasn't the one who did that shit to her or the other women.

"One is my mom, isn't it?" I look over at him and see the look he's giving me. It's a mixture of pity and anger. The only reason I can see him being angry is because we've become friends.

"Yeah. They want to exhume her body to gather evidence that wasn't recovered originally."

I blow out the breath I didn't realize I was holding. "What more could they find. The detectives on her case didn't find anything to point to a killer. What makes us think we can find anything now?" I ask sounded exhausted.

My mind is running through a million different scenarios, all of which she could have died from. After she had left me to live with my dad, we didn't hear from her. It had been a few years until I got word that I needed to come identify the body. At thirteen, I wasn't in the state of mind to do something like that, but my father didn't give me a choice. He refused to go and ID her. He told the detective and me that she deserved what happened to her.

"I don't know man. But what if we find something?" He takes a long pull from his beer and then starts to mess with the label.

"I doubt they will find anything. It's a lost cause. I've looked

for years into her case, and I haven't been able to find shit out." I say bitterly. I should be happy that we are going to have a chance to look over this case, but part of me doesn't want to. It brings back a lot of bad memories, and I'm not sure if I'm strong enough to go through them again.

Canaan and I spend the next few hours talking about random shit and drinking beers.

CHAPTER FIFTEEN

Elijah

The minute I walk through River's door, I can tell something is off. I've been here a shit load of times and never noticed the decorative plate that is by the door. It's on the ground now and smashed to pieces. A few pieces of her mixed matched furniture are moved around from their normal spots.

I dash towards her bedroom, and when I come to the doorway, I stop dead in my tracks. I feel Seb run straight into the back of me. His force causes me to go through the doorway and closer towards where River is. She's sitting on the edge of her bed. The sheets are all messed up, and I can see the black mascara smeared on her cheeks.

Walking towards her, I kneel down in front of her and cup her face with my hands. "River," I whisper softly. Her soft cries feel like I'm being stabbed in the damn chest. I should have been here for her last night. I shouldn't have let her go out alone.

I turn to see Seb behind me, but he doesn't say a word. He just stares down at her.

"River, I need you to tell us what happened," I say as gently as I can. I'm furious that someone even put their hands on

her. My eyes scan over her face, and I notice the slight swelling. They continue their scan, and I see the marks on her neck. She has a couple scratch marks on her neck and arms. "River," I say a little more harshly.

Her eyes snap to mine, and when she finally sees me, she wraps her arms around my neck and cries on my shoulder. I can feel the anger radiating off of Seb, but he continues to watch us. He doesn't once say a word, and it makes me nervous. It's been a while since I've seen Seb this mad. He can typically keep his temper in check.

"Babe, I need for you to tell me what happened," I whisper in her ear. She cries harder, and I pick her up to move her. When I look down at her bed, I see some blood. My grip on her tightens, and I move out of the room with her.

"River." Seb's voice comes gently from behind me. I sit us on the couch, so she's straddling my lap. He takes a seat next to me, and she slowly turns her head to look at him.

"What happened?" Her bottom lip trembles as she watches him, but doesn't say a word. "River," he says again.

"I should have…" she trails off for a second before she starts again. "I should have gone home with you Seb. I'm so sorry." She starts to cry again. I pull her to my chest and let her sob against me. Her whole body trembles and I hate that something happened to her. It reminds me of the shit that Anslie went through a few years ago.

"Baby, you didn't do anything wrong. Whoever put his hands on you is the only one that did something wrong." He states running his hand down her back. When I look over at him, I can see the rage burning in his eyes.

"Who was it River?" I ask. She shakes her head no, and I

have to keep myself from saying something that I regret. I want her to tell us the truth so we can handle it. If she doesn't, I know that Seb is going to search this fucker out, not caring who he hurts in the process. Right now, we don't need that type of attention, especially with the Feds questioning us.

I spent the next couple of hours just holding her. She cried off and on, but never said another word.

When I try to move, her grip on me tightens. "River," Seb says softly. "Come here." She looks over at him and then back at me for a second. He opens his arms for her, and I watch her slowly make her way towards him.

His hand goes to the back of her head, and he pulls her smaller body into his. I watch them together for a few minutes before I get up from the couch and try to find something that tells me who the fuck did this to her.

Walking towards her room, I see the messy bed and blood again. I want to kill the bastard for even putting his hands on her. Fuck. I run my hands through my hair and take a seat on the edge of her bed. She doesn't deserve this shit. I should have protected her better. I close my eyes and take a deep breath. Just as I'm about to get up, I feel her phone vibrate against my ass.

Grabbing her phone, I turn on the screen and see an unknown number. She has three missed calls from the number and a text message. When I click open the text message, I see something that pisses me off to no end.

It's a picture of a hand ripping at her clothes. The other hand is on her throat pressing down on it. It looks like she's struggling to breathe. Her nails are digging into his arms as he holds her down. Grabbing my phone out of my pocket, I dial Trace and tell him to find me all the information on the number.

"I'll call you back in ten." He states before he hangs up. I

walk out of the room towards where my brother and River are still sitting. He's whispering in her ear, but I can't hear the words. Whatever he's saying is calming her down, so I don't try and ruin that. I want her to feel safe here. Hell, I don't think I'll be letting her stay here alone again. I won't let this bastard come near her again.

"Seb," I murmur quietly. His head turns towards me, a protective look on his face. I flash him the screen, and the rage in his eyes turns murderous. When her head turns towards me, I pocket her phone and walk a little closer. Running my hand down the back of her head, I try to think of something else. I feel like I've failed her. I know she won't think of it that way, but I do. I've promised that I would never let anything happen to her since the day I met her.

"We need to get out of here. I don't want him coming back with her here." Seb nods his head in agreement. "I'm going to grab her some clothes and shit I know she can't go anywhere without. We can take her to my place."

I don't wait for an answer this time. I walk back into her room and grab her duffle bag, filling it with enough clothes for a few weeks. After that, I move to her bathroom and shove her makeup and shit inside too. By the time I've gathered most of the shit she brings with her to my place, I walk back towards the front room to see them both standing up. Her whole body looks uneasy, and I hate seeing her like that.

She's the type of girl to not take any bullshit. She doesn't care if you don't like her and she sure as shit doesn't back down from anything. To see the fear in her eyes right now is gutting. That isn't the girl I know. She might be in there somewhere, but she's not the girl standing in front of my brother right now.

"River, you're going to ride with Seb." She slightly nods her head, and he wraps his arm around her tiny frame.

"Come on babe," he softly says, leading her towards the front door where she leaves her flip-flops. Once she puts them on, she slowly walks with him towards the bikes. I lock up her place before making my way over to them. I stuff her bag into my saddle bag and watch as Seb gets on his bike before helping her on behind him. "Hold on to me." His voice is still low and sweet.

Watching the way he is with her right now lets me know that he does care about her. He may say that he's not going to touch her because of me, but now I know how much he really does care about her.

We make the short ride to my place, and I unlock the doors for them. I grab my phone and see my old man's number on the screen. "Hey pops," I answer, pushing the doors open and letting them pass me. Seb takes River towards the extra room, and I shut the door behind me.

"Who the fuck are you looking into?" he bites out. Trace must have told him about the number I asked him to run. Motherfucker.

I run my hand through my hair and tug at the ends. "Some fucking dick that hurt River."

"What the fuck do you mean someone hurt your girl?" I sigh. I swear, no matter how many times I tell everyone that River and I are nothing more than friends, no one believes me.

"She's not my girl," I groan. I hear the door close softly, and I watch as Seb makes his way towards me. "She went out last night, and I think she hooked up with someone." I watch Seb's eyes darken, and a growl erupts from his throat. "He hurt her. She has some scratches and bruising. She isn't saying anything about what happened. I think she's in shock. Seb and I brought her to my place where we are keeping an eye on her."

"Why the fuck isn't your girl under protection. We told you

boys to protect the women and children," he yells at me.

Seriously, last I checked I was a grown ass fucking adult. I didn't need my dad telling me how to run my life. "It happened last night or early this morning. The fucker has photos of it. Not sure if he has anything else. He sent the photo to her phone after she didn't answer his phone calls." I feel the anger radiating off my brother now.

I hear her gasp, and I wince at the sound. Both of our heads turn in River's direction. She's pale as a fucking white sheet. Just as her legs are about to give out, Seb makes three long strides towards her and grabs her body, pulling her to him. He whispers something in her ear, and she wraps her arms around his neck, squeezing him tight to her.

"I don't give a fuck what you say, I will find the bastard that hurt her and make him pay," I growl. My eyes watch as Seb all but carries River back towards my extra bedroom.

"Fine. Let me talk with Cason before I sanction this," he says quietly. I hear my mom's voice in the background, and I know he's only getting quiet because she's in the room.

"Sweetheart is that one of the boys?" She asks near the phone. He grunts out a yes and then her sweet loving voice gets on the phone. "Hey, baby boy." She says like she didn't just see me a couple days ago.

"Hey, mom," I answer. My eyes never leave the door that they disappeared behind.

"How are you doing?" I know what she's asking, but I don't want to answer her. Hell, I'm still not even sure exactly how I'm doing. In reality, all I want to do right now is head back over to Spencer's place. Hell, I don't even care if we fucked; all I really want to do is hold him. Having him in my arms last night and this morning was the first time I've ever felt like I was right where I belonged.

"I'm figuring shit out." I finally answer her.

I can hear her smile in her voice. "I'm glad baby. I just hope you don't wait too long to find what you're looking for."

"I'm working on it, mom," I say with a grin. I instantly think about Spencer, and I know that I need to see him tonight. Seb is here with River, and I can probably slip out for a few hours without them saying anything.

"I love you baby boy. Can I talk to Seb?"

"He's with River right now." I can hear the smile in her voice when she tells me how excited she is to hear that. She's been hoping they get together ever since I told her I was gay. We say our goodbyes, and I promise to bring River over when she's feeling up to it. When I hang up with her, I send a message to Spencer, telling him that I'm dealing with something, but that I'll come by later.

CHAPTER SIXTEEN

Spencer

I'm in bed already half asleep when I hear the soft knock at the front door. Opening my eyes, I throw the blanket off of me and stumble my way towards the door. After the beer, I went straight for the hard shit. All the talk about my mom and the new case had me fried, and the only thing I wanted to do was get drunk.

By the time Canaan said he was heading home, I was three sheets to the wind and horny as fuck. When Elijah sent me the text saying he was on his way, I knew I had to sober up. I poured a bunch of coffee down my throat and was just about to give up on him showing up when my eyes started to close, and the knocking began.

Checking the peephole, I see the sexy biker that I've been fantasizing about since he left me this morning. As soon as the door unlocks, he pushes it open the rest of the way so he can walk through it. His hand grips the back of my head, and he pulls me in for a heart-stopping kiss. If he wasn't holding me up, I'd be in a puddle at his booted feet right about now.

He doesn't release me as he closes the door behind us. The locks click, and I let him lead me towards my room. Some of the alcohol is still in my system, so I don't even think about what we are doing, I just go with it. Feeling his rough hands on my skin makes my dick hard, I want nothing more than for him to fuck me right now. I need him to fuck me right now.

As he pushes me back on my bed, his hands run down my naked chest. His lips trail down my skin, and his hands grip my sweats. He quickly works them down my hips and down my legs. He tosses them somewhere behind him, but I don't even care. The only thing I can focus on at the moment is him pushing his way between my thighs.

His hands grip my hips, and he pulls me closer to the edge of the bed. When he leans over my body, I prepare myself for his kiss. His lips are bruising against mine, and I can only assume that whatever happened earlier, it's affecting him.

His fingers trail along to tops of my boxer briefs, and he slips a hand inside. His fingers wrap around my length, and he starts to work me over quickly. It doesn't take him long to have me panting and moaning his name out. I want him so bad that I'm aching everywhere.

"Fuck me," I grunt out. His eyes meet mine and search them for a second before he even moves. My body is cold when he leaves me to go to my drawer. I turn my head to watch him as he slowly makes his way over to it. I hear a quiet buzzing come from over where he's standing, but he doesn't even acknowledge it. He grabs what he's looking for in the drawer before coming back over to me.

He pulls his shirt off as he moves, tossing on the ground. He tosses the lube and condom on the bed next to me, still silent. I don't even think he's going to say a word tonight. Something about that doesn't sit well with me. Maybe something happened to one of his brothers.

He sheds his jeans and boots quickly before he grabs my boxer briefs and pulls them down to discard them with the rest of our clothes.

I watch him as he runs his palm up and down his shaft, rubbing his fingers over his piercing. My eyes are glued to where his hand is. I can't do anything but stare. Fuck he's beautiful. The ink that sprawls along his one arm and up his shoulder is breathtaking. His hair falls into his face, and he continues to watch me as he pleasures himself. He bites his bottom lip, and I have to move towards him. I have to have my hands on him.

Before I can touch him, he pushes me back on the bed and moves between my legs. He reaches over to grab the lube before slathering his fingers with the smooth liquid. He tosses the bottle back on the bed and steps away from me. "Stomach." He growls into the room. I get to where he wants me without thinking twice. Maybe it's the alcohol, maybe it's the look in his eyes that makes me give in to his wants.

His hands spread my ass cheeks, and I feel his finger runs along my ass crack. It doesn't take long for him to slowly start to slip his finger inside of me. He's impatient, something I've never seen from him in the few times we've seen each other. It's almost like he's trying to forget about something.

He adds a second finger and starts to slowly scissor his fingers in and out of me. I groan and push back on his fingers. The feeling is so damn good that I don't even mind that this is more for him than it is for me. After he gets me worked up to the fucking edge, he removes his fingers from me. I can't help but whine when he takes his fingers away.

"Eli," I whine. His hand comes down on my ass in answer. He doesn't say a word still. The room is silent except for the sound of the condom wrapper. The sound of the condom being rolled on brings a chill to my spine. I can't wait for him to fuck me. Part of me is craving it. Shit, who am I kidding? He's starting to become a drug – one that I crave even when I'm in the same room as him.

"I'll give you what you need. I'll always take care of you, babe," he murmurs. He grabs the bottle and squirts a good amount of lube on his hand before running it along his length. Fingers start to probe me again, I feel the cold liquid being spread around my ass before he slowly sinks his finger in me again. My hips buck back against him, and I hear his slight intake of breath. "I love seeing you like this." A hand comes down on my ass again, and I have to bite my lips to keep from yelling out.

He rubs the head of his dick along my crack, and I can feel his piercing through the condom. As soon as he starts to push his way in, I start to feel shit I shouldn't. I shouldn't be falling for this guy. Not after this short period of time and definitely not if he's a biker. His hips slowly thrust in and out, gaining inch by inch with each thrust. Biting my fist, I try to keep out from screaming. Fuck he feels so damn good.

When he fills me completely, he leans his hard, strong body against mine. His lips trace the edge of my ear and his breath fans over my skin. "Being inside you makes all the bad shit disappear." His teeth trail along the skin of my cheek and down to my neck where he bites down on the tender skin.

I can't help but moan at all the sensations and the way his words make me feel. "Fuck," I grunt out when he starts to move in and out of me. Each slam of his hips is rough, but I crave the feeling of him taking me this way. Each thrust feels amazing, I can feel myself getting harder. Reaching down, I start to run my hand up and down my shaft. One of his hands comes around to play with my balls. The feel of his lips on my neck brings pleasure that I've never experienced before.

His hand wraps around my neck, and he pulls my head back onto his shoulder. His lips find mine, and he kisses me until I

can't breathe. I can't even function with all the things I'm feeling. My balls tighten, and I'm going to come. Before I can even say the words, he's running his rough hand up and down my shaft, pulling my orgasm from me.

He plunges into me harder and deeper, almost at a frenzied pace as his orgasm hits him. His grip on my neck tightens, and he kisses my mouth roughly as he comes. I swallow the sounds of his grunts as he rides out his orgasm, slowly his motions until his body melts into mine. "God." He moans into my neck. His lips trail a line along my collarbone before he pushes himself up and off me. "I love the feel of your tight ass." He gives it one last slap before he pulls the condom off and tosses it in the trash can close by.

I stand up and turn to face him. His eyes look almost hollow for a split second before they change to the light gray color they naturally are. "You okay?" I ask running my hand down the side of his cheek. He leans into my touch, and one of his arms wraps around my waist, pulling me to him.

"I'm better now that I'm with you." His tongue swipes over his lips, and he leans down to bite my lower lip. I watch his features, and I notice that he's hesitant, almost guarded. He doesn't want me to know whatever happened today.

"You taste like beer." He says with a grin. I shrug and start to move towards the bed.

"I may have had a couple." I finally answer when he doesn't let me go. At my answer, his grip loosens on me, and I am able to get in bed. He follows me and cuddles up to me. His arm wraps around my chest as he kisses my shoulder blade.

"Shitty day?" he asks. His voice is like a salve being applied to my broken soul.

"You have no idea." I murmur. His arms tighten around me, and I close my eyes, letting the rhythm of his heart thump against my back.

"Sorry babe." He mumbles, burying his face into my neck. I run my fingers along his arm that is wrapped around me. He doesn't say anything for a few minutes, but the silence is comfortable. "I would have stopped by when you sent me that message, but my best friend River sent me a text that wasn't like herself." He pauses, and I feel him blow out a breath.

"She said she needed me. If you knew her, you would know she doesn't need anyone. She's got a mouth on her sometimes and can handle herself. I taught her to fight in high school. So to see her message, I knew something was wrong." His lips find my skin again, and he presses a soft kiss where his mouth is.

"Is she okay?" I ask. My profiler instincts kick in, and I want to help if I can. I know I haven't told him what I do for a living, but I know as soon as I do, he's going to bolt. If he's an outlaw biker, there is no way we can be together. I haven't had enough of him to lose him already. I need more time.

"I don't know. Physically, she'll be fine. Mentally, I have no fucking clue. She isn't talking. I think she's in shock. Some asshole hurt her and I wasn't there to protect her as I should have." His words hit me hard. Thoughts of my little brother hit me, and I have to hold my breath. Closing my eyes, I try to focus on something other than him. I need to stay strong.

When I get my composure back, I turn in his arms and face him. "You should be with her, not here." His eyes close and when they open again, I can see the anger and hurt in them.

"My brother is with her. She hasn't left his side since we picked her up at her apartment."

120

I can't imagine what he's feeling right now. If it were me, I would be out there trying to find out who the fuck hurt her. Just as I'm about to offer my help, his phone starts to go off again in his jeans pocket.

CHAPTER SEVENTEEN

Elijah

The ringing of my phone breaks the moment we were just having. I'm not one to spill my fucking guts to someone, much less someone outside of the club. Well, except River. Just thinking about what she went through is tearing me up still. Fuck. I can only think that I failed her somehow. I should have been there. That fuck head is going to wish he never preyed on her when Seb and I are done with him.

The ringing doesn't end even after I ignore the first call. Sighing, I get up and grab the phone from my jeans. Looking at the screen, I hit the answer button and slide back into bed with Spencer. "Yeah?" I grumble.

"When you coming back?" His voice sounds tired, and I get it. Sitting up watching her is probably the hardest thing for him right now. Even though Seb doesn't admit it, I know he has some major feelings for her.

"In the morning," I answer roughly.

"You heard Pops; we aren't supposed to be out alone. What if the Feds pick your ass up?" He's getting pissed, and part of me doesn't blame him. If it were the other way around, I'd be

pissed too.

"Nothing's going to fucking happen. Chill out. I'll swing by my place to check on her."

"Don't be a fucking idiot. We have the family to think about too. It isn't just about us anymore." He spits into the phone.

"You think I don't know that shit? You may be in love with River, but she's been my best friend for years. Even when you were too stupid to see her, I was there for her. So don't try and make me feel bad. Fuck you Seb." I don't bother waiting for his response. I hang up and set the phone down next to me. Putting my arm over my eyes, I take a few calming breaths.

As soon as his arm drapes over my side, all the anger vanishes. He calms me. Call me stupid, but I could fall in love with him without any effort. Lying on my back, I watch him. He moves closer to me, and his face leans over mine. "If you need to go, I get it." Instead of answering him, I reach up and wrap my arm around his neck, pulling his face down to mine.

"No. I'm right where I want to be." The minute his lips hit mine, I can breathe again. The suffocation I was starting to feel disappears and the only thing I see is him.

"Elijah," he whispers.

"Spencer." I kiss him lightly. "Just give me this. I need this." I look into his eyes, and after a few seconds, he nods. I pull him down on my body, and he rests his cheek on my chest. "Thank you," I whisper to him.

"I'd do anything for you." His voice trails off almost like he wasn't ready to share that information with me.

"You have no idea," I reply, before closing my eyes and falling asleep to the sound of his soft breathing.

The bright sunlight shines through his open window. Groaning, I roll over onto my back. Spencer moves with me and cuddles into my side. His eyes are still closed, but his warm body pressed against mine feels like heaven.

"I don't want to go to work." He says kissing my chest.

"Then don't." I murmur, running my hand down his back.

"I have to. After leaving early yesterday, I'm now way behind." His breath warms my skin. I think of some of the things I can do to him before I get going, but my phone has different ideas than me. Grabbing it from next to the pillow, I see Seb's name on the screen. "What?" I grit out. He's fucking called more in the last night than he's done all our damn lives.

"I can't get her to stop crying. I don't know what to do." He sounds stressed as fuck, and I kind of feel bad for him.

"I'm on my way." I hang up before he says anything else. I don't want to hear anything else. I need to get to her. If I can at least calm her down, then shit will get better. I hope it gets better.

I turn to look at Spencer, but I can already see the understanding in his eyes before he even says "Go." I lean towards him and press my lips to his. His scent fills my nose, and I know that I'll never tire of that smell.

"She needs you. Go be with her." I force a smile at his words. It kills that she's going through this. She's strong; I know she will make it through this even stronger than before.

"Thank you," I whisper. I'm headed into unchartered territory, and I have no fucking idea what I am doing. I don't know if he is really going to be here when I finally come back, or if he'll still see me when I have the blood of another man on my hands.

He has no fucking clue the man I am on the outside. Right now he's only seen the me that is deep down inside of me, not the man my family and brothers see every day.

Getting out of his bed, I grab my jeans and pull them on quickly along with my tee and boots. When I finally slow down for a second, I see him wearing a pair of jeans low on his hips. His tan skin on display, the bars from his nipple rings are like beacons trying to bring me back to bed with him. Walking towards him, I wrap an arm around him and pull him to my body.

"I'll call you later," I mumble against his lips. His arms wrap around me, and he pulls me closer to him.

"You better." A soft smile forms on his lips and I can't help but grin back at him. He's slowly grabbing hold of my heart in a matter of days. I'm so fucking screwed.

Before I pull away, I kiss him once more before I grab my phone and head out the door.

When I finally get back to my house, I see Seb standing on the porch. He looks stressed the fuck out, and I can only imagine the shit he's feeling. He's got the same look on his face that Brant did when Anslie was raped and abused by that crazy fucker. "You okay?" I ask when I put my kickstand down. The engine goes silent, and I walk over to him.

He rubs his hands over his face a couple of time before he finally looks at me. "No. Seeing her like that…" He trails off and shakes his head. "How the fuck was B able to look at Ans without wanting to fucking kill everyone who had ever hurt her? Right now, I want to fucking kill every bastard that has ever looked at her wrong. I want to gut the bastard who put her in this spot." He blows out a breath, and I feel the same anger he does.

"We are going to make the bastard pay for what he's done

to her. As for Brant, I'd talk to him if I were you. He's going to be your best bet at figuring this shit out if you want her like I know you do." I put my hand on his shoulder for a second before I make my way inside.

I follow the sounds of her crying. When I find her in my bed, I see the tears streaming down her face. She's never been one to sleep in my extra room. She demands that she shares my bed. Walking towards her tiny body that's curled up on the bed, I can see that she's shaking. The more she cries, the louder she gets. Climbing into my bed, I lie on my side and face her.

"I'm right here babe," I whisper. Her head tilts up slightly before she scoots her way towards me. As soon as she's close enough, I pull her body into mine. She buries her face into my neck and starts to sob. Running my hand down the back of her head and down her back, I do my best to comfort her. I don't know how to deal with this shit.

I tried my best to not have to deal with the emotions like this. I hate seeing her cry.

I lay with her for what feels like minutes, but turns out to be hours. When Seb comes back, he looks like he's showered, but that's it. He still looks like he hasn't slept and I hate that for him. He's never let a girl take over his emotions before.

"She asleep?" He finally asks after a few minutes of watching her in silence.

"Yeah," I respond. The sound of my own voice is foreign to me.

"Dad and Prez are here. They brought Anslie with them." I nod and slowly pull out of her grasp. I need to talk to them. They brought Anslie for a reason. They are going to try and get her to talk to River, and hopefully help her through the shit she's going through.

126

"Let's go figure out a plan." I get up from the bed and press a kiss to her cheek lightly. She stirs a little, but doesn't wake up. Heading for the living room, I see all three of them sitting on the couches. Anslie looks like she might cry and our father's look pissed.

"How is she?" Anslie asks first.

I sigh and run my hand down the back of my neck nervously. I don't even know how to explain how she's doing. Before I can answer, Seb is. "She's doing shitty," he bites out. His voice laced with anger. "She is either stone cold silent, or crying her damn eyes out."

I see Anslie flinch at his tone and Prez goes to say something, but she waves him off. "Don't forget I know what she's going through. I get that you're mad, but taking your attitude out on me doesn't help her." With that Anslie gets up and storms down the hall. I shake my head. She's right, she is the best bet at making sure River gets the help she needs or talks to someone.

"Don't ever disrespect my daughter." Prez barks out when Anslie is out of sight and in my room. River doesn't know Anslie's story, but I think she will appreciate knowing that Anslie is someone she can talk to.

I watch as Seb tries to gain his composure. He's falling apart. He doesn't know what to do and hell, neither do I. "We get that you care about your brother's girl, but –." Before our father can keep talking, I stop him.

"She isn't my girl. She's been in love with Seb for almost as long as we've been friends." I sigh. I'm tired of trying to convince everyone that she and I aren't together. Shit, I know it would be easier if I was. I run my hand through my hair, and I see both my father and Prez stare at me like I'm fucking crazy.

"Does your mother know?" My dad finally asks.

"Yeah. We talked about it. I told her that River is in love with Seb and she was happy, ecstatic even." I wince when I see the look on Sebastian's face. He doesn't do love, that much I know. I don't see him confessing his feelings for her at any time, but at least he knows where she was before all this shit has gone down. I can only imagine how he's feeling now that he knows that he's the reason she's been careless.

"I'm the reason for her crazy antics. All because I kept trying to keep her home instead of out in the club trying to find a piece of ass." Seb says as he pales and I look towards my bedroom door.

CHAPTER EIGHTEEN

Three Weeks Later

Walking into my house, I shut the door behind me and make my way toward the kitchen. Elijah and I have a date night planned tonight, and I'm dying to see him. We've been together most nights when I get off work, but the last few nights he's been busy with his brothers.

He doesn't say much about it, but then again I don't push it. We've talked about our careers a little over the last few days, but I still can't bring myself to tell him the truth. He might hate me if I tell him I work for the bureau. Plus he's a biker. I'm still not a hundred percent sure that he's not part of a club.

I know the clubs around Henderson and Las Vegas, and none of them are the ones you want to cross.

The only thing I've told him about my work is that I work in an office and I'm on call a lot. He never questioned me about it, so I didn't say anything. There have been times where we both have been called away right when we were getting ready to go out or just relax at home. I've even had to leave just as we sat down to dinner that he cooked for me.

I hear a slight knock before the door opens. Walking through the kitchen, I hit the living room just in time to see Elijah strutting in the entry way. His tattooed arm is on display, and I love the way the color contrasts against his white tee.

When he sees me, he makes his way towards me. His gray eyes never leave me as he eats up the distance between us. His arm rises just before he reaches me and he cups my cheek. His lips fall down on mine roughly. As he pulls me into his body, I can't help but moan into his mouth. I can already feel his dick pressing into me the moment we touch.

Every time I see him, it's like the first time. He's fucking beautiful. Just the sight of him turns me on. Hearing the sound of his voice is one of my favorite things. I had no idea what I was getting into when I met him, but fuck am I glad that I did.

His lips hover above mine, and I look up into his eyes. "Fuck, I've missed you." A playful grin spreads across his lips.

"Right back at you biker," I smirk. His eyes get a look in them, and I know exactly what is going to happen next.

Before he can grab me, I take off running towards the bedroom. If I don't change right now, there is no way that I'll be leaving this house tonight. The last time this happened, we didn't end up eating. Instead, the only food we had was each other. Boy, I don't regret that either because it was the best sex of my life.

Who am I kidding, every time we've had sex has been the best sex of my life. He doesn't do things easy ever. He makes it to where I feel him for the next few hours every time.

I can hear his boots on the ground behind me as he closes in on me. An arm wraps around my middle, and I'm being pulled back against his hard body. It doesn't take long for him to put one

of his hands at my throat. The minute his lips hit my skin, I can't help but moan. The feel of him against me my body fucking amazing and I could die a happy man right now.

His hand around my stomach starts to slide down, and I suck in a breath when his fingers slide across the top of my jeans. His fingers tighten against my neck, and I moan into his ear. "Fuck." He undoes my jeans quickly before shoving his hand inside of them.

Fingers wrap around my dick tightly. Groaning, I press my ass back into his strong body. His hand slowly starts to move up and down my shaft a few times before he releases me and removes his whole body from mine.

The feeling of cold air where his warm body once was is torture. I want nothing more than for him to fuck me right now. Hell, I don't even care if he took me right here in the middle of the doorway. I'm so damn horny that he could fuck me anywhere, I wouldn't mind.

His hands grip my hips for a brief second before he's sliding my jeans down my thighs. One of his hands goes to my lower back, and he leans me forward. His hands continue until they stop on my ass cheeks. I can feel him behind me as he slowly sinks to his knees. The crack of his hand hitting my ass causes me to jump slightly.

A moan tears from my lips. His mouth caresses my skin next. Each little nibble and suck turn me on more than before. Putting my hands on the doorframe, I spread my legs a little to give him access.

I love how willing Spencer is. He doesn't question me when I do shit. He lets me take control and doesn't bitch about it. These last few weeks have been like heaven in the crazy life I live. I know by now that I should know more about him, but I like the surprise. We don't get all mushy when it comes to how we feel about each other either. We go with the flow of the relationship we've sort of fell into.

Never in a million years did I think that I'd be spending most of my nights wrapped up with him. It's not the type of man I am. I fuck them, and then I leave them that night. I never stay for longer than necessary, but for some reason I hate walking away from Spencer.

Grabbing the small bottle of lube from my pocket, I flip the cap and put a healthy amount onto my hands. Squirting some onto his ass, I run my wet fingers between his cheeks and slowly work a finger inside his tight hole. I watch as his back bows down a little while I'm working my finger in and out of him slowly.

As I add a second finger, he's pushing back against my hand, just begging for more. His whimpers turn me on so damn bad. Fuck. I almost can't wait. I need to take him now.

Standing up, I undo my jeans and push them down to my knees. I run my hand up and down my cock and lube it up before I stand behind Spencer and slowly press the head of my dick to his perfect little hole.

Leaning over his back, I pull his face up and lick my way up his neck. I gently bite down on the tender skin of his neck before moving to the spot right under his ear that he loves. I know it drives him crazy, so I always run my tongue over the skin right there.

"Fuck me, Eli," he moans. The back of his head is resting on my collarbone. One of my hands is at his neck, and the other is

rubbing the tip of my cock along his puckered hole. When I start to slowly sink inside of him, he sighs. The feel of his walls squeezing me feels fucking amazing. Each deep thrust causes him to move forward. His hands brace on the casings of the door, and he slams back into me just as hard as I'm ramming into him from behind.

Each thrust brings me closer to the edge. Sex with Spencer is always satisfying. I never feel like I need to fuck anyone but him. Shit, I wouldn't even mind being tied down to him for the long haul. I shake my head to rid the thoughts of being tied down already. We don't know each other enough to even be thinking about that. We just barely started fucking without protection a few days ago, after our tests all came back clean.

Spencer's body starts to shake, and I reach around to grasp his dick. I slide my hand up and down his shaft, applying just enough pressure to bring him to the edge quickly. His moans fill the room, and soon his warm cum is shooting on the ground in front of us. I start to thrust into him quicker as I chase my own orgasm.

Grunting out my release, I cum inside of him. His body collapses, and I have to hold him up. "Fuck," he mutters quietly. I kiss along the back of his neck before I pull him up to standing height. I slowly pull out of him and pull my jeans up enough to walk into the bedroom.

Leading Spencer over to the bed, I pull his shirt off and toss it on the ground next to us before pushing him back onto the bed. I grab his pants and pull them and his shoes off, tossing into the already growing pile of clothes.

I pull my shirt over my head as I make my way to the bathroom to grab a cloth to clean the floor. Once, I get his cum wiped clean from the floor, I toss the cloth with the other clothes. Shucking off my jeans, I make my way towards the bed.

Spencer's eyes never leave me as I get closer. Climbing into his bed, I pull his naked body into mine. "I know you were looking forward to going out, but three days without you means that I'm not letting you out of bed until I get my feel of you," I say, kissing his neck.

He cuddles into me, and I rest my hand on his heart. These moments are the ones I've come to live for the last few weeks. Having Spencer in my arms before I fall asleep at night keeps the demons away. It keeps the guilt at bay over the death of Raef. The thought of being happy even a fraction of the same as my parents keeps me coming back, even if I don't want to admit it.

"What are you thinking about?" He asks, cupping my cheek.

I lean into his touch and close my eyes. He doesn't need to know all the crazy shit that runs through my mind on a daily basis. Instead, I tell him a white lie. "I was just thinking that my mom would love you."

He blushes slightly, and I lean forward to press a kiss to lips. "She would?"

"Yeah. She's all baby fever right now because of my older brother B, but she's been dying for me to meet someone. She wants me to be happy." I smile sadly. I hate that I won't be able to tell them about Spencer. There is no fucking way my brothers or father will understand.

"Can I meet her?" His question catches me off guard. I try to ignore it, but he asks it again.

"As much as I want you to, it probably won't happen. They won't understand." I frown, and the words feel bitter as they leave my mouth. Do I want him to meet my family one day? Yeah. Do I think that it will be a good idea? No.

My family won't understand, plain and simple. They won't greet him with open arms, and we probably won't ever be able to live the happy life that I wish I could. Secret. All we will probably ever be is a secret.

"So you're going to keep me your dirty little secret?" He has a playful, yet serious grin on his face. I don't know if I should feel bad or be glad.

"You won't be a secret to everyone." I murmur. "I know it sucks for you, but trust me when I say this… My father and brothers won't understand." I cup his cheek and slowly caress his skin. "I don't want to subject you to how they might react."

"I can handle myself, babe," he responds. I lean forward to claim his lips once more.

"I know you can. I'm just not ready for it." I close my eyes as I think about the ridicule I'd be subjecting him and myself too.

"I get it. We can go at your pace." He kisses my forehead and wraps his arms around my neck, pulling me on top of him.

CHAPTER NINETEEN

Spencer

Two Months Later

I've watched stake out videos and ran through tapes of interviews that the guys have collected over the last few months. Everything has been slow going lately at work. The case we are building isn't one that we can rush, and I hate it. I like being able to start one case and close it within a week or two. Long cases aren't my strong suit, especially if we think my mom was a victim years before.

The memories of the night I had to ID her are coming on stronger and stronger every day that we work the case. All of our other cases have been put on hold until we find the bastards that are involved with this shit. I want to take them all down – every last fucker that is involved. I've been digging deep into the Souza Cartel without the permission of my superiors. As much as I know I'm breaking protocol, I don't care. I want to know if they were the ones responsible.

My eyes scan the screen, and my heart falls. The side of his head looks familiar, and I get my confirmation as soon as he turns his head and looks right at the camera. Closing my eyes, I

feel my heart start to race. No. This can't be right. There is no fucking way that he would be involved.

Canaan comes and takes a seat next to me, putting his feet up on the desk. "Why you look like you saw a ghost?" He asks. His eyes scan the screen and then turn back to me.

"Who is that?" I point to the guy he's interviewing in the video.

"Nick Insico." His eyebrow raises, and he waits for me to ask something else.

"What does he do?"

"He's the Vice President of the Wayward Saints MC," he states slowly. "Why do you know him?"

I close my eyes and take a deep breath. "Who's that with him?"

"One of his sons," he says without hesitation.

I feel my face pale. There is no fucking way. "You know his son?" He finally asks when I don't say anything else. My eyes shoot back to the screen, and I see his crooked grin that I've seen almost every day for the last few months.

"My sexy biker." Those are the only words that fall from my lips. I put my head in my hands and suck in a breath. I slowly try to calm my heart rate. I feel like my heart is going to beat out of my chest at any fucking minute.

"Oh fuck." he blows out a breath, and his feet come off the desk. "You mean you've been fucking one of the Saints?" I nod my head, but don't look at him. I can't even process this shit right now. "He never said anything? You've been fucking for a few months now. Not once has he slipped about who he was?"

I shake my head no, and I try to drag in a deep breath. Fuck.

A knock on the door brings my head up only to see Dixon standing there. He has a concerned look on his face, and I know that he's heard what was said. "Can you use him as an informant?" His question throws me for a loop.

"No. There is no way he'll turn on his family. No fucking way." I state.

"We don't need him turning. We just need information on the other players. We can build a case against the Saints after the fact." I feel my stomach turn. I can't do that. I can't let something happen to Elijah. No fucking way.

"Call him. Get a night with him." I feel sick at the mention of me using him. He doesn't deserve that shit. He's a good guy, I know he is. I can't even fathom him being involved in something this sickening.

"I can't," I say hoarsely.

"It's your job." Dixon grits out. I know he wants to close this case and shit, so do I, but I don't want to use Elijah to do that. I've fallen hard and fast for him. Just knowing that I can come home to that every night makes the long days I've put in here worth it.

I close my eyes, and when I open them again, I see both Dixon and Canaan staring at me. "You can help find the people responsible for your mother's death." Dixon's words are like a kick in the teeth. Closing my eyes, I nod my head and pull out my phone. I need to find answers. I hate this.

Dialing his number, I put it on speakerphone and wait for him to answer. "Hey, babe." His low growl sends my dick into a frenzy. I can't let him affect me right now.

"Hey. Can you come over tonight?" he doesn't say anything for a second. I haven't had to ask him to come over lately. He just shows up and somehow sneaks into my house while I'm in the shower.

"Everything okay?" He sounds concerned, but I can't let him find out that I know who he is. When I look over at Dixon, I can see the hardness on his face. Canaan looks almost hurt that I have to do this.

"Not really. I just need to see you." I state softly.

"Yeah, I'll be there the normal time. Is that good?" I hear a few people talking in the background, but I can't make out any words.

When I look back to Dixon, he mouths 'now.'

"Can you come now?" I feel sick. I can't believe I'm about to betray his trust for this case. I'm falling in love with him, and now I'm going to ruin everything.

"Yeah. I'll head that way in ten. I have something I have to finish up with my brother." I blow out the breath I was holding.

"See you soon." I murmur before hanging up the phone. My heart breaks and I feel like I got the wind knocked out of me.

"I want to know who their contact is with the drug cartel. You get me the information, and I'll keep him out of jail." I stare at him blankly.

"And what about his family?" He gives me a hard look at my question. I know how much he loves his family. We've talked about it a few times. He would do anything for them, including taking a bullet. All of a sudden something clicks. A few weeks ago, I asked him what the hardest thing he's ever had to do. When he told me about one of his best friends dying, I could see the pain written all over his face. He kept saying that he wished it was him that took the bullet for his friend's dad. He told me about Raef and how much he had to live for. That his life was cut short in order to save his own father.

He also told me that his friend's father was about to become a father again and that he took the bullet, so his sister didn't have to grow up without a father.

I watch as Dixon leaves and I don't bother with the look that Canaan is currently giving me. Instead, I grab my laptop and search the cases for the death. It takes a good twenty minutes before I find the case. I scan over the notes and reports and see that the victim's girlfriend was the one interviewed by the cops. It also notes that the President of the Wayward Saints is his father.

There were other bodies found around the victim's, and they were known members of the Souza Cartel.

Grabbing my bag off the desk, I grab my phone and start to walk out the door. "Spence," Canaan calls from behind me. I turn to look over my shoulder at him. "Be careful. You have no idea if this shit will go sideways. I'm sure he cares about you, but you're not family." I nod my head before I walk out the door.

If I tried to get words out, I'm sure they would be along the lines of not wanting to do this and that if it gets fucked up, I'm going to lose the only man I've ever loved. Shit. Love? Do I love him?

I contemplate this shit the whole way to my house. It's a little after noon, all I can think about is seeing him. I shouldn't want to see him when I know I'm just going to end up hurting him and myself in the process.

By the time I get to my front door, I hear his motorcycle roar down the street. I turn to watch him pull into my driveway and put his kickstand down. He pulls his helmet off and straps it to his

bike before stalking towards me. His hands are on my face, and he's pulling me in for a long deep kiss. When he pulls away slightly, I can see the lust in his eyes. As much as I want to fuck him right now, I can't. I can't betray him and fuck him.

"What's wrong baby?" he asks. His eyes burn right through me, and I hate the feeling it brings. What was once an amazing feeling now makes me sick.

"Let's go inside," I whisper. I can't even look him in the eye anymore. He follows behind me, and I unlock the door quickly. I have a feeling that what I'm about to say is going to ruin every single moment between us. Every sweet kiss, every tender touch. I can't think about it, or I might just say fuck my job and run away with him.

The door closes behind him, and I hear the lock click into place. When I turn to face him, I see the uncertainty written across his features. "You are a member of the Wayward Saints MC." I choke out around a dry throat. His eyes narrow on me, and I take a step back. I'm not afraid of him, but I know that he's going to take a step towards me and demand I tell him what I know about him.

"I feel like I'm at a disadvantage," he says quietly. He takes a step towards me, and when I go to move again, he reaches out and snags me by the waist, pulling me into his body.

"You are," I say quickly. The sooner I get this out, the sooner I can close this case and figure out who killed my mom.

"Why don't you tell me what you know about me," he growls.

"I know you are the son of Nick Insico. You have three brothers; Brantley Insico, Jason Insico, and Sebastian Insico. Your mother is Emily." I pause right there. His eyes darken with anger, I know that he's trying to figure out how I know this.

"Your brother Brantley is with the Wayward Saints' President's daughter. They have twins together and a new little one." He continues to stare at me. "He's the next in line when your father steps down." He closes his eyes for a second. When he opens them again, I see the red hot anger in them. It doesn't get him to release me though. If anything, I can feel his fingers dig into my back.

"Why do you know about my family?" I close my eyes for a second and try to gather my thoughts and a deep breath.

"I'm part of a crime task force." My voice doesn't even sound like my own. I feel my heart break at the pain in his eyes.

"How long?" His voice is dark, and I know he's trying to figure out what was real and what was fake.

I don't answer him. The answer won't fix any of this. I'm supposed to find out information on their contact with the cartel, and I can't even give him a straight answer. He releases me and walks backward towards the door. "You let me fuck you to get information? What do you want to fucking know? Huh?" he yells. His voice echoes off the walls in my entryway, and I wince at the answer.

He takes a step towards me and reaches out, grabbing me by my neck. He doesn't squeeze, and part of me knows he won't actually hurt me. "Don't fucking lie either." He backs me up until I hit the wall. His hand tightens around my throat, and part of me wishes he would just get it over with if he's going to actually hurt me.

"Tell me, Spencer! What the fuck are you looking for?" His face is right in mine, and I hate the feelings that are running through me. I want to kiss him and tell him that I won't let anything happen to him. I want to tell him that I'm falling in love with him. I

can't do either of those things.

"I just found out who you are today. My boss overheard something I said to my partner." I swallow, and I feel his hand tighten. "He wants me to get you to turn on your family." His fist flies at the wall next to my head, and I continue to stare at him.

"I should have fuckin' knew better." He shakes his head and squeezes tighter before he lets go. "I won't sell out my family ever. I'm not a rat." He pushes away from me and turns to walk out the front door.

"Elijah." I plead. He turns to look at me, and I see the shit I did to him. "I wouldn't let you anyway. I don't want to bring your family down. I want the people who killed my mother. The same bastards who left that body on your guy's doorstep." He turns to face me this time.

"What do you know about that?" he growls.

"I know she was killed by the same people who killed my mother." His face softens a bit, but I still see the anger simmering below the surface.

"We didn't fucking kill her," he growls. I know that. I don't tell him that. He probably wouldn't believe me anyways.

"We have the tapes from your guy's cameras." My voice isn't my own, and I know that it's because of how I feel about him.

"Then what the fuck do you want from me, Spencer?" He yells. I flinch at his tone, and I just watch him. He can't stand still as he waits for me to answer him. He's pacing in front of me, and every time he looks at me, the anger in his expression gets worse.

"My boss wants to know who your contact with the Souza Cartel is." His eyes flash, and he stalks towards me.

"You seriously think we are messed up in that shit? You apparently didn't listen to a damn thing I've ever said to you. We are clean. We don't do that shit. If anything, that fuckin' cartel is the one who dropped that bitch off on our doorstep." He stares at me with contempt.

"Why would they be after you?" I ask.

"Because we ruined a deal of theirs. They work with the damn Vegas mob. My brother died at the hands of the mob." His face darkens, and he turns away. "Fuck." He grits out. He told me something he didn't want me to know.

"Elijah." His head turns towards me, and he narrows his eyes at me.

"What?" His voice is rough, and I don't know if it's because of the emotions or what.

"I should have told you sooner." I look towards the ground and wait for him to say something.

"I knew you were too fuckin' good to be true. Don't fuckin' call or come near me again." He bites out. I feel the rejection in every inch of my body. The cold way his voice snaps at me causes me to pause. I knew this was coming. I should have just kept my mouth closed. I wouldn't be losing the one thing I care about. The sharp pain in my chest wouldn't be trying to claim me.

He doesn't say another word as he makes his way towards the door. I don't even bother stopping him. I know he's pissed and I get that. I would have been pissed if it was turned around. As the door slams shut, I whisper into the empty entryway, "I love you, Elijah."

144

CHAPTER TWENTY

Elijah

The emotions that are running through me right now are fuckin' intense. I never expected this shit. I never expected to feel that much anger and hurt. He's a damn cop. Stalking towards my bike, I throw my helmet on and straddle her. Cranking the engine, I don't even wait before I take off.

He knows everything about my family. He was fuckin' using me. *Shit.* I can't even think straight right now. Instead of heading home, I make my way to the bar. I know that I shouldn't, but I can't bring myself to go home yet. Not with all the shit that's been going on. The Feds have been back to interview Prez and a few of the members for whatever bullshit they are trying to get us on.

He was part of this case. He knew and never once said a damn thing. Pulling into the parking lot, I shut off my bike and make my way inside. As soon as I walk in, I see that it's dead. It's not even after two in the afternoon yet. Part of me is glad that I don't have to deal with the crowd yet. I just want to get fuckin' drunk, and fuck someone else until I get him out of my system.

As soon as I sit at the bar, the bartender comes over to me. He's cute in a pretty boy sort of way, but he isn't Spence. I shake my head; I'm done thinking about him. "Hey baby, what can I get for you?" He asks, eyeing me like I'm his next victim.

"A bottle of Jack," I reply. I scan my eyes over him, but he does nothing for me. Almost like he can tell my mood, he doesn't stick around. He goes and grabs me a bottle and sets it in front of me with a shot glass.

Cracking the bottle open, I swig straight from the bottle. I can see the look of concern from him as he makes his way over to the other side of the bar. I grew up drinking. As soon as we hit sixteen, we learned how to drink. Mom hated it, but our old man didn't mind. He knew we were all going to wind up in the life, so he allowed it.

I spend the next few hours just taking swigs from the bottle. My mind is a cluster fuck of emotions, and as much as I want to call him, I don't. He played me. *Goddammit*! I thought he was someone different – someone who actually gave a fuck about me. God, I'm a fucking idiot.

As the bar starts to fill up, I continue to drown my sorrows in a new bottle of Jack. A hand on my shoulder brings my attention to two twinks standing behind me. These two are slim, and baby-faced. I don't even think they are more than twenty-one, but right now I don't give a fuck. They aren't Spencer, but that's probably why I get up and follow them to the dance floor.

Standing in the middle of the dance floor, I have these two all fuckin' over me. Hands running over my body, I force out all images of Spencer out of my head. I just let these two have their way with me. I'm not feeling anything at the moment so they could do anything they want.

I have one of them behind me, grinding up against my ass and the other one rubbing his ass against my dick. The liquor makes me forget who I have touching me. My dick is hard, and I

want nothing more than to behind him over something and fuck him into tomorrow. An arm wraps around my neck, and I'm pulled into a kiss.

His lips don't feel like *his*. They feel way too soft and thin. I imagine it's Spencer standing in front of me. My dick hardens even more, and I get the urge to wrap my hand around his throat. As much as I want to make it rough and hard for him, I don't. Part of me wants to hurt him for the shit he's done, and the other part just wants me to claim him. Make him mine in every damn way possible.

"Elijah." I open my eyes and see Spencer standing there staring at me. He's pissed, and I'm glad he is. Fuck him. "Get the fuck away from him," he growls at the twinks. I smirk at Spence and watch him push the one in front of me away. The other one moves away from me when he sees the look Spencer gives him.

Spencer wraps his arm around my neck and pulls me closer to him. "That isn't your style." He murmurs loud enough for me to hear him over the music.

"You don't know shit about me." I bark out. I know I'm just fucking pissed at him still but fuck. Just having him this close to me right now makes me think of all the shit I want to do to him. Instead of waiting for him to make a move, I slam my mouth down on his.

I push my tongue into his mouth, and I kiss him like it's the last time. Hell, it probably will be. There is no way in hell I can even think about letting my family get locked up because I was fucking a Fed.

My hands run down his back, and they grip his ass, pulling his lower body into mine. His moan is low and throaty. He wants me just as much as I want him right now. Just thinking about him while the twinks were all over me made this even worse than I planned. At least with them, I wouldn't be fuckin' the enemy.

"Let's go," I demand in his ear. I bite his earlobe and drag my teeth over the soft skin. His hands on my arms tighten, and he nods his head in agreement. "I'm going to fuck you."

He follows me out to his truck, and I push him up against the door. His head connects with the window, but he doesn't say anything. His eyes never leave me. Pushing my hips into him, I kiss his mouth roughly. "There's a hotel down the street. Meet me there."

His eyes darken, and I bite his lower lip, pulling it into my mouth. "Okay," he says quietly. He and I are about to have one last fuck before I disappear.

I release him and push myself back and away from him. I watch as he gets into his truck. Making my way towards my bike, I straddle her and start the engine. His truck starts up, and I watch it as he pulls out of the parking lot.

The ride is short and the minute I stop, the only thing I can think of is getting him naked. I go through the motions with my bike before making my way over to his truck. He's leaning against it, staring at me. I walk straight for him and grab his face, pulling him into me. I kiss his lips roughly before I pull away and walk towards the lobby.

Entering the dingy little area, I walk straight for the guy standing behind the desk. "Can I help you?" He asks with an eyebrow raised. I pull my wallet out of my back pocket and pull two bills out.

"I need a room. Without it being on the books." He looks at me strangely before I flash the two bills. He grins and grabs a key off the back wall.

"Room twelve." His smile widens when I take the key and

hand him the cash. "No one comes near the room until the morning." My voice is dark, and he nods his head, not caring what I'm about to do in there.

Walking out, I make my way towards the room. I don't even say a word to Spencer. I still don't have anything to say to him. A fuck, that's all this is going to be. I'm going to use him like he used me.

Unlocking the door, I push it open, and the smell of the room hits me. It smells just as bad as it fuckin' looks. Growing up in the MC life, I've been in my fair share of dumps, and this doesn't even hit the top of shitty places I've stayed.

The minute the door shuts behind me, I don't have to turn around to know he followed me. He wants me just as much as I want him. The pull between us is undeniable, but I'm not letting that cloud my judgment right now. I want answers first. I want to know why he would do this shit. Why he let me fall for him when he knew that he was going to just fuckin' use me for a case.

"Why?" I demand. I don't turn around because I can't look at his face as he lies to me.

I can feel him get closer to me, but I refuse to look at him. "I was forced to. I tried to get out of it because I was already falling for you. I didn't know who you were until today." His voice breaks slightly, and when I turn around to face him, I see the truth in his eyes.

"Yet you still called me and asked me to come over even knowing what you knew about me." he nods his head and reaches out for me.

"As much as I want answers, I want you more. I would give this shit up all for you Elijah." I shake his grip on me off. I start to walk further into the room, and when I turn to look at him again, I can see the rejection on his face.

"I fuckin' trusted you!" I yell. "You fuckin' lied about what you did for a damn living." He looks to the ground for a second before he looks back up at me. "You told me you worked in a damn office. How the fuck can I trust you now? Huh, Spence?" I slam my hand into the wall, and he flinches.

He slowly walks over to me and puts his hand on my cheek. I have to close my eyes from the intimate touch. It means nothing now. Fuck, but I want it to mean everything like it did the other night when I fucked him slowly. When all this shit finally made sense to me and I realized something more powerful. I realized that I loved him.

I was in love with the sexy, nerdy man who made me feel like I was the most important person to him. It was almost like I hung the damn stars for him. Who am I kidding, I still love him. He only wanted one thing from me. Now that he has it, he doesn't need me. I sure as hell don't need him.

I'm a biker, and he's a Fed. Shit between us will never be more than that.

CHAPTER TWENTY-ONE

The look in his eyes breaks my heart. I knew I'd hurt him when I told Dixon that I'd do what I had to in order to get information. As much as it pained me to say those words, I said them. Part of me wants to find the answer, but not at the price of losing him. Digging into the case the way I have been is dangerous.

Some of the case information is missing, and I can only assume that there is someone on the inside giving information to the Souza Cartel. I haven't said anything to my team yet because I don't know if any of them are involved. Hell, I can't even tell Elijah. I've hurt him, and he could be the one giving information about me to them.

No, he wouldn't do that. I can see it in his eyes, he still cares about me.

Walking over to him, I put my hand on his cheek. His eyes close and I move closer to him. "I'd give all this shit up for you Eli. I can find new work. Being with you these last few months has made me feel more alive than anything else I've ever done." His eyes open and he nails me with a look of anger.

He moves so quickly that I don't have a chance to back away. His hand goes to my neck, and I'm being pushed into the wall. Face to face, I stare into his eyes. He's fighting with his emotions, and I know it's eating him alive right now. "I fuckin' hate what you've done to us," he finally whispers. Instead of responding, I close my eyes and suck in a breath.

When I open them again, I see the pain. "I love you," I whisper. The timing is wrong, I know that, but if this is the last time I see him I won't take of chance on him not knowing. I watch his expression change a few times. Love, anger, regret all flash through his expressions.

His grip on my throat tightens, and he cuts off my air. He pushes me back into the wall, and I just continue to watch him. Even with him cutting off my air, he doesn't scare me. The bad boy biker has nothing on the man underneath it all. He slowly releases his grip, and I cough out a couple of breaths. Backing up from me, he shakes his head. He's fighting with something in his head, and I know that it has to do with me.

Rubbing my neck with my hand, I keep quiet and let him work it all out. He knows where I stand; now he needs to tell me where he stands. I just hope like fucking hell that I'm worth it to him.

When he comes back towards me, his words surprise me. "Fuck it." His hands grip my face, and he kisses me like it's the last time. His fingers dig into the back of my head, and he pulls me to him. His hands slide down my back, and he grabs my ass, squeezing it roughly. We are all lips and teeth. His hands grab the bottom of my shirt, and he rips it over my head, breaking our contact.

I grip the bottom of his tee and yank it up and over his

head just as quick. His fingers start to work on my jeans, and he gets them undone and starts to push them down my thighs. My dick is already hard and springs out of my jeans. I kick my shoes off to help him out, and he drops to his knees before me. He takes me into his mouth quickly and runs his fingers around to my ass.

A finger slowly probes me before he pulls back and spits on his hand. He gets back to sucking my dick, and his finger slips into me. He doesn't take his time like he normally does. This time it's urgent. Suddenly, he stands back up to his full height and starts to undo his jeans. He pushes them down to his knees and spits on his hand to lube himself up.

When he's done, he grabs my neck and pushes me back against the wall. His lips descend on mine, and he's kissing me like he's starved. Spinning me around, he pushes my face into the wall. His hand on my back keeps me from moving. His other hand grabs my hip, and he moves me where he wants me.

One slow thrust and he's inside of me. The intrusion is painful, but part of me gets off on the pain, almost like I deserve it for breaking his trust. His hand grabs the top of my hair, and he pulls my head back, kissing his way down my neck as he picks up his pace behind me.

The feeling of him pounding into me hard from behind without the condom feels so fucking good. His piercing adds to the feeling, and I'm glad we got checked. The force of his hips hitting my ass runs me into the wall. No words come out of his mouth, and it stings. I know as soon as he gets off, he's walking away. I knew it the moment I saw him in the bar with those twinks all over him. I've lost him.

I moan as the feeling of him taking me rough and hard. I'm on edge and I know I'm going to come soon. He just feels too fucking good inside of me.

His grunts in my ear have me closing my eyes and just feeling it instead of trying to keep myself from falling apart.

Bracing my hands on the wall, he moves his hips, so his thrusts hit my prostate. It doesn't take long at this angle for me to fall apart. He grabs my arms and pulls me back into his body as I groan out my release, spraying my cum on the wall in front of me. It doesn't take much more for him to come. His moan is low, and I know this is it. He's leaving.

Elijah rests his head on my shoulder for a second before he pulls out of me and starts to pull his jeans back up. I lean my forehead against the wall. I can't watch him walk out that door. No fucking way. "Thanks for the fuck," he states. He sounds pissed, but I ignore that. I get he's mad. I don't blame him really.

I hear him pull on his shirt and start to walk away. When the door opens, I hear his voice one last time. "I love you, Spence." Closing my eyes, I feel the tear slide down my cheek. The door closes softly behind me, and I turn away from the wall. Sliding down the wall, I close my eyes and put my head in my hands. I hear the phone in my jeans ring, but I can't bring myself to answer it. I don't want to hear that I failed my team and I don't want to hear Elijah tell me how much I hurt him. I rather just sit here on the floor of a dirty hotel room and pray that this was just a damn dream.

It takes a good hour before I'm able to pull my ass up and off the floor. The pain in my chest still hasn't let up. The ache is constantly throbbing as I try to breathe. My lifeline is gone. He walked away. Pulling my jeans back on, I grab my phone out of my pocket and see Canaan's name on the screen. Hitting his contact, I wait for him to answer.

"Spence," he says sounding out of breath.

"Hey," I answer morosely. I don't even feel like talking to

him right now. Hell, I don't feel like talking to anyone right now. I'd be okay just hiding out in my place until I can drink away the memory of Elijah.

"You need to –" The door to the room breaks apart as four men come rushing in wearing masks. One of them tasers me, and I lose control of my arms and fall to my knees. I drop my phone somewhere on the shitty carpet before I pass out.

Waking up, I try to move my arms, but I remember what happened. Looking around the room, I see that I'm in a garage of some sort. Nothing looks familiar. I try to sit up, but I can't. My hands are tied behind my back, and my ankles are tied too. I'm on my shoulder, and the pain that shoots through it is almost unbearable.

The door to the room opens, and I see a few men shuffle inside. The door closes with a loud bang, and I flinch at the ringing it causes in my ears. "Spencer Hart." The voice brings chills to my spine. "You just couldn't leave it alone, could you?" He steps out of the shadows, and I see his face. The older gentleman standing in front of me is the head of the Souza Cartel. I've seen his picture everywhere when I was doing research on them earlier.

"Cat got your tongue?" He laughs. His laughter is more of a cackle, and I feel my whole body tense. I've read about some of the things he's done, but gotten away with. If he is behind my mother's death, then I can only imagine what will happen to me."

"You know son, I remember your mother. She was a real beautiful woman." He runs his hand over his beard, and then he takes a few steps closer to me. "It was a shame what had to be done." He makes a tsk'ing noise before he squats down in front of me. "I didn't expect you to be a fag." A wicked grin creeps over his face, and I see the craziness written all over his face. "I can't wait to have my way with you."

His hand reaches out to caress my face, but I turn my face. There is no way in hell I'll let him touch me. Closing my eyes, I pray that Canaan can find me. He had to of heard what happened. Even if I die today, I at least got one more night with Elijah. He may never come looking for me again, but at least I heard him say the words that I've been dying to hear fall from his lips.

He loves me.

"I can only imagine what your boyfriend's family will say when they find out that he's a fag too." He chuckles at himself, and I just stare at him. "Bikers aren't gay. Maybe they'll put him down, and I won't have to worry about what you two gossiped about during pillow talk." A finger reaches out towards my lips, and I bite down on it.

His screams fill the small room, and a gun comes down on the side of my face. My head hits the ground with a lot of force, and I see stars from the impact. A fist comes down on my face next, and I grunt out from the pain.

Blood starts to run down my forehead and into my eyes. "I'm going to find that bastard and kill him instead. How do you like that?" He stands up and kicks me in the stomach once before he starts towards the door.

Once the door slams shut, I wipe my eye the best I can on my shoulder. Opening my eyes, I see that the room is completely bare. The walls look run down, and the cement slab has stains all over it. I can only imagine what they use this room for.

He knows about Elijah. Fuck. We talked about it before, so I know what he hasn't come out to his family and that he wasn't going to. I hated his decision, but I also understood it to some extent. My father doesn't know about me being gay either, but then again I haven't spoken to him in years. I haven't gotten a call

that he's died yet, so who knows what shape he's in. Hell, I don't even really care anyway.

I just wish there was something I could do for Elijah.

CHAPTER TWENTY-TWO

Elijah

Leaving the way I did is eating away at me. I love him. No, I don't. Shit, yeah I do. If I'm fucking honest with myself, I love him more than anything. Coming to a stop a couple miles outside of Las Vegas, I turn around and head back to the dump I left him in.

The whole ride my head is consumed with thoughts of him. Did he lie to me? Yeah. Do I believe that he just found out about me, maybe? There is too much shit running through my mind right now. I don't know what to fuckin' believe.

I make it back to the hotel faster than normal, and I see his truck still sitting in the parking lot. Getting off my bike, I make my way towards the room and see the door busted in. Running the rest of the way to the room, I make my way inside and see words written on the wall above the headboard.

HE'S NEXT

My body tenses as I look around the room. I see his phone sitting on the ground, and I see that there is a number still on the screen. Grabbing it off the ground, I put it close to my ear. "Who is this?" I bark out. There's a slight pause before a voice comes on.

His rough voice fills the phone, and I tense with his words. "So help me god if you are the one who took Spencer, I'll find you and gut you."

"Naw, I saw him earlier when he came to the bar and pushed the twinks off me, but he was still here when I left."

"Elijah Insico." I close my eyes at the mention of my name. Of course, he knows who I am. He must be a Fed.

"I didn't have the pleasure of knowing your name before I came back for Spence." I grit out.

"I'm his partner, Canaan Devlin. We are on the way to the scene." I curse under my breath.

"Yeah, then I'm not sticking around. You're just going to pin this shit on me." I hear voices in the background, and I freeze. When his voice comes back on the line, his words keep me glued to where I'm currently standing.

"Our boss will give you full immunity if you help us find him." The words settle in the pit of my stomach. Help the Feds. The club will fuckin' kill me if they found out I took a deal to save Spencer.

"Only if you give my whole family and club the same deal. I want it in writing too." I hear them whispering to each other some more before he gets back on the line.

"Deal." He breathes. "We will be there in a minute." I set the phone down on the dresser in front of the bed and take a seat on the bed. This shit is going to be a fucking nightmare. Instead of hanging around with the blood on the wall, I walk out of the room just as they are pulling into the parking lot.

They all jump out of the SUV quickly and make their way towards me. "I'm Dixon Tate, and I'm the leader of this task force.

I know that you and Spencer were having a relationship." His eyes scan over me, and he motions to the men around him. "This is the rest of the team, Canaan Devlin, and Fox Harmon."

Each man nods his head at me before they start to move towards the room. I follow behind them. As soon as they walk into the room, they freeze. The words on the wall are the only thing they are looking at.

"Do you know what this means?" The one in charge demands. I shake my head no and watch them all for a second. I don't fucking trust them. There is no way in hell I'll be doing anything to help them until I have the deal in writing. "You want that deal, then you better start fucking talking." He growls.

I raise an eyebrow at him and stand my ground. There is no fuckin' way I'll be letting a Fed tell me what to do. "I need the paper in my hand before I help you. I can find him on my own, without your help and get him back before you can even figure out who did this shit." A grin pulls at my lips. They probably think I'm lying, but I'm not. I can get the information they are looking for, but I have to go to Prez to get it. I'm going to have to out myself to save Spencer's life.

"I can't get it right this second. I need to go to the higher ups." He frowns.

"Then I can't help you. I'm going to go and find him," I state was I walk past them. All three of them look at me in shock and I know that they are pissed I'm not helping. I can't jeopardize my club and family. They are all I have.

Making the drive back to the clubhouse, I think about what I'm going to say. My whole fuckin' life is about to change and either they will accept me this way, or they won't.

The minute I pull into the lot, I see a few of my brothers standing around bullshitting. Shit is just about to get cracking here,

and I know that most of the members are going to be around. Walking inside, I see my old man and brothers standing together. As I walk up, their heads turn towards me.

"Where the fuck have you been?" Seb grounds out. He's pissed I left all of a sudden earlier and left him with River. She's been slowly starting to get back to the girl she was before, but that's only because we went after the fucker that the photos came from. I still don't know who took them, but I will find out.

"I need to talk to you guys and Prez." My old man eyes me for a second before he pulls his phone out and sends out a text.

"Let's head inside." He says motioning to the church doors. I follow behind them, and I hear booted steps coming behind us. When I take my seat, I see Prez whispering something in Brant's ear. He nods his head and sends out a text.

When the door shuts, I take a deep breath and prepare myself for the thing I've keep close to the vest for a number of reasons. Bikers aren't gay. My family wouldn't understand. My brothers wouldn't understand. People wouldn't understand. Fuck.

"What's going on kid? It's not like you to request a sit down." Prez says from the head of the table.

"I need some help finding someone." I stop there because I don't know exactly how to say the rest.

"Is it a woman you've claimed?" My old man asks this time. I shake my head no and they both frown. "Then who the fuck is it?"

"His name is Spencer." Their faces scrunch up in confusion, and I take a breath before I continue. "He..." Shit, I can't do this. My phone starts to buzz in my pocket, and I see a message from an unknown number.

Unknown: *Let me help you. He's my partner and I'll do anything to help find Spence.*

I look back at the men surrounding the table. My family, my brothers. "Spence and I have been seeing each other." I finally push the words out of my mouth. Gasps fall from their mouths, and when I look at my father, I see the disappointment written on his face. Biting the inside of my cheek, I try to focus on the problem at hand. "He's been looking into the death of the bitch that was dumped on our doorstep. He's a Fed."

Sebastian stands up and pushes his chair back from the table. "That's what you've been doing while I sit at your place taking care of River? You've been fucking a damn Fed!? Seriously, we have enough shit on our plates, and this is what you bring us?" He doesn't catch the part where I admitted I'm gay. Not yet. The rest of them did, because they are all sitting there staring at me like they have no idea who I am.

"This Spencer guy..." My old man says quietly. I look over at him and see him trying to figure it out. "He means something to you?"

"Yeah, I love him." I choke out. If their looks could kill me, I'd be six feet under already. "I think the Souza Cartel is behind it." I try to get their attention off the fact that I'm gay and in love with a man that's a Fed.

"How long have you two been together?" Prez's voice is dark, and I know why he's asking. He wants to know how long I've been feeding him information about the club to him.

"Couple months, but I've never once told him who I was. He just found out today." I take a breath before I continue. "He never got any information from me. I wouldn't put the club at risk. I broke things off with him when I found out who he was." I look down at my hands and close my eyes. If I hadn't left him there,

this shit wouldn't be happening right now.

"What do you want us to do?" Brant says from beside me. All heads turn to him, and he doesn't take his eyes off me.

"Brant." Our old man says, but Brant holds his hand up.

"Do you get how fucking hard that must have been for him to admit that shit to us? He's gay, not stupid. You taught us better." Before he can continue, the door opens, and Dom, Bentley, and Robbie walk in the door. The take their seats around the table, and all eyes are back on me.

"Fill us in," Dom says from his seat. His eyes move around the table, and I see the questioning look on his face when he looks back at me.

Sighing, I just say the words. "I'm gay." Their eyes widen, and I push back from the table. I start to pace behind the table, and I see the looks on their faces. They don't accept it, but I expected that. Before anyone can ask any questions, Brant saves me again.

"Can we get back to that later? Spencer?" He says more as a question. I nod my head, and he continues, "He's been taken. We need to get him home." My phone dings again and when I sneak a glance, it's the unknown number again.

Clicking the message I see that he's here. Fuck. Just what I fuckin' need. More fuckin' shit to deal with.

"His partner is here. He wants the same thing I do." I state. All eyes on me narrow except for Dom and Brantley.

"Can we trust him?" Dom asks, surprising the shit out of me.

"He's a Fed. I've never met him until today. If Spencer

163

trusted him, I trust that." I state. I don't back down when Prez gives me a look of suspicion. We don't trust outsiders. I know this – we all know this.

"Bring him in. If he crosses us, a bullet will be put in his head." Prez finally growls. I nod my head quickly and make my way out the church doors and towards the parking lot. When I see a black Chevy truck in the parking lot, I make my way towards it.

Since the drama with the Fed and the local cops, we've had the bar closed to outsiders. It's not hard to figure out who doesn't belong.

CHAPTER TWENTY-THREE

Spencer

My breathing has turned shallow, and I don't know if it's from the kick to the ribs that the bastard left me with, or the fact that he let his cronies have their turn with me afterward. Coughing, I see the red blood on the ground next to my head.

I'm starting to feel lightheaded, but I can't let them win. I want these assholes to pay for what they did to my mother.

When the door opens, I look up to see Esteban Souza, the head of the Souza Cartel walking back into the room. "So you ready to give me the information I want?" His voice is rough, and I know he's tired of asking me.

"I don't know shit. You can keep beating me, and I still won't be able to answer you. We fucked, we didn't talk about what he did." A kick to my leg makes a loud cracking noise and I know for sure he cracked the bone in my thigh. I yell out in pain before I rest my head against the cold ground.

Closing my eyes, I try to focus on something other than the pain that is now radiating through my whole right leg. "Undo him," he barks out. One of the guys comes over to me quickly and cuts the rope around my wrists and ankles.

I watch the men as they start to come closer to me. I don't let them know that inside I'm fucking terrified that I'm never going to get to see his face again. Closing my eyes, I think back to the last time I was truly happy.

The knock at the door signals that he's here. Getting up from the bed, I make my way towards the front door. The minute I open the door, he pushes it open and pushes me into the wall. His mouth is on mine before I can even greet him. His tongue is pushing into my mouth, and I'm relishing in the feel of his body pressed up against mine.

When he finally breaks our kiss, I groan in frustration. I want more, but he's moving inside the house. I frown as I close the door behind me. Walking into the living room, I watch as he drops down onto my couch, making himself comfortable.

Walking over to him, I cross my arms and tap my foot against the ground. "What babe?" he asks, smirking up at me.

"Don't be a dick." I huff out. We are supposed to go out to the bar we met. We are supposed to be going to have a night out. A night of fun. Typically we stay holed up here, making out and getting a little freaky. Okay, a lot freaky.

"I'll give you a dick." He wraps his hand around my thigh, pulling me down on him. I straddle his lap and wrap my arms around his neck. His lips trail down the sensitive skin of my neck and towards my collarbone. His hands slide up and under my shirt, causing me to gasp at his cold fingers.

"Mmm." I moan, throwing my head back, giving him better access to my throat.

It doesn't take much for me to grind against him. Feeling him harden underneath me is the greatest feeling. Knowing that I have the power to bring him to his knees is the best compliment. "Fuck, you keep doing that, and I'm going to give you my dick before we go out. Hell, we probably won't even make it out once I get started with you and your sweet ass." His hands grip my ass cheeks, and he gives them a squeeze.

A kick to the ribs brings me back from the memory. I suck in a labored breath as I roll over onto my stomach. The pain is radiating throughout my whole body. Before I can even try and fight back, someone grabs me and pulls me up.

The weight I have to put on my leg is so excruciating that I almost black out. I feel a prick on the back of my neck, and soon something rushes through my system. I can't see straight, and everything is getting hazy. "Now fucking tell me what I want to know about the Wayward Saints." He demands. He grabs my face in one of his hands and squeezes my cheeks together. The only thing that does is make me laugh. I have no idea what the fuck they just pumped into me, but I'm kind of digging it.

"Tell me what you know about your boyfriend." He yells. I start laughing again, and I get a blow to the face in return. The back of my head hits one of the assholes holding me up, but it doesn't get me to talk. "Now!" he barks out.

"He's got a big dick." I laugh. I can't help it. It's the truth. "I especially like when he fucks me against the wall. So fucking hot." A grin tugs at my lips and I take another punch to the face. I feel the blood start to drip down my face again. There's nothing I can do to clean it off, so I just shake my head, hoping to get some on the douche bags holding me still.

"He told you about himself. Now give me the information I

want." He punches me in the gut, and if these guys weren't holding me up right now, I'd be on the ground. Coughing, I try to catch my breath, but it's no use. I start coughing up blood again and spit it on the ground.

No matter what they do to me, they won't get any information from me. The truth is Elijah never told me a thing about his biker life. When he was with me, we lived in the moment and never looked past each other. Who he was outside of his time with me wasn't important to me. I only wanted his attention when we were together. Work and family didn't matter as long as I had him with me.

I knew he had friends and family at home, but nothing more than that. I knew what happened to River and that's only because he came to me after it happened. He broke down in my arms a few nights after it happened. He told me how he should have been able to protect her, but he was too busy trying to get my attention instead.

"I'm fucking waiting," he growls. I shrug my shoulders the best I can, but I don't really move like I was hoping I would. I feel a prick in the back of my neck again, and my body feels lighter than ever. My head spins, and everything looks like its fucking changing colors. Holy fuck, what did they just shoot me up with?

The spinning gets worse, and I can barely keep my head up. The walls no longer look that dingy color that I thought before. Now they seem to be bright colors. Shit. My legs give out completely, and dumb and dumber are now holding my entire body weight.

I'm not a big guy, but them holding me doesn't seem like a walk in the park, especially since it's all dead weight.

The door opens, and I hear whispers that seem louder than their yelling. "He isn't giving us anything. Maybe he didn't

know anything about the Saints. The drug should be working." The new man says frantically.

"Get me something that will work! I want the fucking secrets he's keeping about his little boyfriend. There is no fucking way he didn't say shit about the damn club." Estaban's pissed and I get why. He thought I would be the one to give him the inside scoop on the Saints, but he doesn't know that I'm just as clueless as he is when it comes to their shit.

Another punch to the gut has my body hunching over even with them holding me up. They drop me to the ground, and I hit the concrete floor hard. The pain in my thigh doesn't even faze me, but I have a feeling that the shit they are pumping into me is the cause of that.

I don't feel the pain, the only thing I feel is lightheaded. I try to keep my eyes open longer, but I can't. My mouth is dry, and the room is going black. Shit. I just want to see his face once more. I just want one more kiss. Right now, I'd take one more word.

As everything goes black around me, I just thank God that I got the amount of time I had with him. He opened my eyes to a love that I never knew was possible, especially with a man like him. A biker with a heart of gold. Sappy, I know.

CHAPTER TWENTY-FOUR

Elijah

"Elijah." His voice carries through the empty parking lot. Bikes are lined up, but not a soul is out here. Everyone is still inside drinking like they normally do on an average night.

I walk over to him and come to a stop. "Why do you want to help us?" I ask, crossing my arms over my chest. If he tries to fuck us over, there will be nothing I can do to stop what they'll do to him.

"He's my partner, one of my best friends. I know he loves you so if he trusts you, then I trust you." He states quietly.

"Your boss know you're here?" I ask. He shakes his head no and sighs.

"If he knew I was here, he'd have my gun and badge. There is no way in hell I'm letting those bastards take Spencer. They'll kill him if they don't think they can get information from him." I nod my head because we know these assholes. They were in bed with the mob that was after Sailor. These were the men that tried to gun us down after Raef killed that bastard who bought his ole' lady.

170

"Let's go. All the key members are in church." He doesn't say anything as I turn and walk inside. As we make our way through the room, people stop and watch. Feds and cops aren't allowed in here unless they are on our payroll. We all know who those men are, and this fed isn't.

Ryder stops him before he can get past the bar area. "Who the fuck let the Fed in?" He growls. I know it's his way of protecting us. He's done a lot of bad shit for the club when we needed it, and there isn't another man I want on my side. We are going to need all hands on deck when we try to get Spencer back.

Turning to face Ryder, I motion for him to move. He stares at me for a second before he finally does. "He's here on a special request. Don't fuck with him or you'll deal with me." I bite out. All eyes on me narrow and I can't help the frustration that is running through me right now. "Let's go," I growl. He continues to walk towards me, and the guys don't say another word. They know that I have the power to make decisions, just not a major one. Family has its benefits.

As we walk into church, the whole room goes silent. Not one person says a word until I shut the door behind the Fed. "This is Spencer's partner. His name is…" I trail off and look back at him. I can't for the life of me remember any of their names.

"I'm Canaan Devlin. I'm part of the Special Crimes Task Force in the FBI." All the eyes in the room stay on him. He doesn't move from his spot, and that's actually a good sign. I'm sure if he went to take a seat, one of the brothers would have snapped his arm or something.

"Take a seat," Prez says from the end of the table. I walk over to my own chair and motion for him to follow. The seat to my left is vacant since Ryder is out in the bar still.

"So what do you know about the Wayward Saints?" Prez

questions.

"Not much Sir," he states. He looks around the room and then back to Prez. "I interviewed Nick Insico a few months ago, but I never learned anything other than you're a family of bikers. I didn't dig anything up."

"That's because we don't have shit to hide. Why is someone trying to get information on us anyways?" My old man asks.

I look over at Canaan, and he looks a little worried. "Well ever since the body of Carissa Phillips was found here at your establishment, it has brought the attention of a string of murders dating back awhile." He looks around the room again before settling his eyes on me. "Spencer's mom was a victim when he was a teenager."

Closing my eyes, I try to not think about it. If this is the same person who has him, then they are going to kill him. No doubt about it. He was probably still digging for her killer, and it could cost him his life. "Fuck." I grit out, slamming my hands down on the long wood table. All eyes hit me, and I press my fingers into the wood, standing up. I need to walk around or something.

"He's been working the case when he has free time. He noticed the same markings on Carissa Phillips that his mom had on her at the time of her death. When Dixon told him to get information from you this morning, I didn't expect this to happen. He refused at first."

My eyes level on Canaan. "Why did he do it then?" He almost looks ashamed of his involvement.

"Dixon brought up his mom." Those five words give me the answer to everything. "He told us you wouldn't give up your family. He knew that without even talking to you. I will do everything in my power to make sure nothing happens to the club too. I just want to

find Spencer. They will kill him if they don't get the information they want. I don't want to have to identify his body if we don't get to him soon enough."

I run my hand through my hair and look to Prez for help on that one. The room as been quiet and I know that it's because they are watching and trying to figure out the next step. We plan for a reason. We want to ensure that one wrong move won't get another one of our men killed.

"You sure it's the Souza Cartel?" Dom asks from his seat next to his old man.

"They are the ones who killed one of your members. They were the ones left at the scene when they took…" he trails off when he sees the look on Prez's face.

"They were the ones behind my son's death?" Prez's face is stone cold angry now.

"From all the evidence I've been over, it points to them. Have you had problems with them in the past?"

"One," Prez states coldly.

"Maybe retribution?" Canaan suggests. Prez and my old man exchange looks and I know there is something they aren't saying.

"We don't have enemies." My old man states. I roll my eyes and shake my head.

"Can we focus on finding Spence?" I demand. I'm tired of this going in circles bullshit. If Canaan is right, they will kill him. If he knows anything about them from his research on his mom's case, he's going to die.

"Fine." My old man states grumpily.

"Where do they hide people?" Canaan asks.

I look around the table and see the expressions on everyone's faces. "Please," I say softly. "As pissed as I am at him right now for not telling me the truth, I love him." My hands go to the table, and I look to my brother Brantley. "I don't want to lose him."

"They have that warehouse off Turner." Dom's voice carries through the silence. I can feel the eyes of my father burning through me, but I don't care right now. All I want right now is to see Spencer one more time. I need to know that he will make it out of this shit alive.

"Let's load up. We take out every one of them." Prez turns to look at Canaan and raises an eyebrow at him. "You okay with that Fed?"

Canaan doesn't even hesitate with his answer, and it brings a smile grin to my lips. "Fuck yeah."

Everyone gets up, and we make our way out of church and towards the arsenal we keep hidden. After the ten of us grab enough ammunition to take out a small army, we make our way out to the van. As we are loading up, a hand comes down on my shoulder. When I turn to see who it is, I see Dom standing there staring at me. He doesn't say anything at first, but after a few beats, he speaks.

"I'm proud of you kid. I get how fucking hard it is to come out the way you did, but just know you'll always be welcome in the club under my watch." He squeezes my shoulder. "They will come around. You're family. Not all the guys are going to understand, but I want you to know I have your back."

"Me too kid. You're my baby brother. They say shit to you, they can deal with me." Brant says before getting in the back of the van.

After everyone loads up in the van, Jase takes us in the direction of the warehouse on Turner Road.

CHAPTER TWENTY-FIVE

Spencer

The room is dark when I finally come to again. I feel like the room is still spinning and I can barely open my eyes. I'm exhausted, and I don't know if it's from the lack of water or the shit they've been pumping into me.

The darkness is deadly silent, and I have no idea how long I've been in here alone. My muscles are starting to hurt again. I try to move my leg, but the throbbing takes over, and I end up on the ground again grunting out in pain.

"Kill him." I hear through the wooden door. I look up and see the handle start to move. "He doesn't have the information we need, so he's no use to us. Find me someone who knows about the Saints MC." I move the best I can in order to keep out of sight of the fucker that's about to walk in the door.

I force myself to stand and wait for the bastard to come in the room. When he does, I hit him in the throat with my elbow. I fall onto him and wrap my arm around his neck. I snap his neck quickly and push my body away from him.

The pain in my thigh gets worse, and I almost black out

from the pain. The room grows quiet again, I try like hell to hear if anyone is coming towards the door. When I don't hear anyone, I slowly make my way towards the wall next to the door. When I press my back against the wall, I hear footsteps coming towards me.

As the doorknob turns, I get ready to attack the next person who comes through the door. Gun shots blast through the place, and I can't tell where they are coming from. I cover my head just as the door flies open. The door hits the wall with a loud thump, and I feel the corner of the door catch my leg. I grunt out in pain, and the person on the other side of the door comes around it and points the gun right at my head.

I throw up a prayer and close my eyes. There is no fucking way I'm going to be able to get out of the way of his bullet. The bang echoes through the room. I try to move as fast as I can, but it's no use. The sting of the bullet tearing through me steals my breath. My mind focuses on Elijah and all the shit I wish I could have told him. I wish I could say sorry to him for calling him and getting him to drop everything and come to my place where I told him that I knew who he was. Where I broke his trust. I feel my body start to get cold, but his voice is in my head telling me to hold on.

My eyes start to close, and I feel my body slump to the side. The voice gets louder, and I try to open my eyes. Hands grip my face, and I feel lips press down on my skin. "E..." I can't get anything else out of my mouth.

CHAPTER TWENTY-SIX

Elijah

Rushing into the old run down warehouse, we take out the guard's right inside the door. Canaan follows me, taking out a man that is coming around a corner. Each man that goes down, I can't help but feel a little better. Yelling comes from somewhere in the back of the building, so we make a beeline towards the noises. I hear more bullets erupt around us as my brothers take out more men.

The sounds of bodies hitting the ground sickens me, but I focus on finding Spencer. I have to find him. He can't be dead. I refuse to lose another person I care about.

"Over there," Canaan says as a shadow catches our eyes. We make our way towards the hallway the guy went down, and I see a door closing. Kicking it open, I put my gun in the door and take a foot to my wrist. The sound of it popping causes me to pause as the pain envelopes me. I yell out just as someone runs right at me.

We tumble to the ground, and I try to buck my hips to get the bastard off of me. His hands go to my throat, and he tries to cut off my air. I reach up and put my hand on his face, trying to

push him away from me. Before he can do anything else, the pop of a gun fills the air around us. Blood splatters all over me and his now limp body rests on top of mine. Pushing him off of me, I get up and grab my gun from the concrete ground. My wrist is fuckin' throbbing, and I can barely make a fist with my right hand.

"You okay?" Canaan asks concerned. I nod my head, and we keep moving towards the back of the room. A door is open, so we continue towards it. The sound of a gun going off urges us to both run towards the sound. Hitting the open doorway, I see the bullet hit Spencer. Tackling the guy, I lay him out on the ground and start hitting him.

I lose control for the first time. I hit the guy so many times that by the time I'm huffing out for breath, Canaan is pulling me off of him. Blood is dripping down my hands and covering my shirt. None of that matters when I look over at Spencer. His body is slumped against the wall by the door. His thigh is swollen, as well as his face and a majority of his body. Blood is seeping through his shirt.

"Spencer!" I hear my own voice, but it doesn't sound like me. "Hold on Spencer." I drop to my knees and press my hands against his wound. The blood doesn't stop, and soon I'm covered in his blood too. "Get a fuckin' ambulance," I scream. Boots start coming towards the room, and I hear my brother's curse under their breath.

"Spence, please hold on," I whisper against his cheek. The tears start to fall from my eyes, and I press my lips to his forehead. I can't lose him. Fuck.

"I need an ambulance, officer down, I repeat officer down." Canaan's voice barely sounds like a whisper as I sit with Spencer. I shouldn't have left him. I should have listened to what he had to say instead of taking off. Regret fills me as I hold him, keeping my hand on his bullet wound, blood seeping between my fingers.

"E..." he whispers. His eyes start to open, but he doesn't see me. His eyes are unfocused before he passes out. I run my fingers over his face, and I smear blood all over him. Putting my head against his forehead, I pray for the second time since I was a kid. I pray that God lets Spencer live. He never answered our prayers for Raef, so I think he owes us one.

Closing my eyes, I try to keep a positive outlook, but I can't. I'm going to lose the best thing I've ever had before I really ever got it. He's going to be gone before I can ever tell him that I love him.

"You guys need to leave," Canaan says from somewhere nearby.

"No, we aren't leaving him." I think Jase growls. "We don't leave our family behind."

"I can get him off, you guys I can't. Just go. I'll keep him protected." Canaan's voice is tight. I've never heard him use this tone with anyone and I can see why Spence likes him. He's protective, and not many can say that their partner went against protocol to help save their life.

"We aren't leaving him." My old man's voice breaks through the tension. "I won't leave my son behind." My eyes close and the tears fall harder. I have to bite the inside of my cheek to keep from crying even more than I already am.

The sirens get louder, and I know that if they don't leave now, they will all be questioned. We will have to answer why we have the guns we have and why we killed these bastards. As much as I want to tell them to leave, I can't.

Part of me is happy that they are still here. It means that they haven't written me off yet.

When I look up, I see the sadness written on their faces. "If we have to go down for killing those bastards who shot Spencer, then I'm not afraid of doing time. We're a family, and I'll always have your back little brother, just like you've always had mine." Brant's words echo through the room. I close my eyes and put my head against the wall. Brant comes towards me and leans down to whisper in my ear so the others can't hear him.

"Fight for who you love. Don't let them tell you it's wrong." His hand wraps around the back of my neck, and he squeezes. "I love you brother." I slightly nod my head.

"I love you too B."

"I need to get them in here without thinking they are going to take fire," Canaan mumbles as he makes his way through the building. It seems like hours before he comes back with the paramedics and the rest of his team.

"We are going to need you to move." One of the paramedics says to me. I nod my head and wait for the medic to put his hand where mine is covering his wound.

I slide out from under him, and when I stand up, I see Dixon, I think, walking towards me. "Elijah." He reaches his hand out, but when he sees that I'm covered in Spencer's blood, he balks. "Thank you for finding him." I nod my head, but don't say anything. One of my brothers comes to stand next to me, and he puts his hand on my shoulder.

My eyes flit back to Spencer as I watch them get him ready to go to the hospital. "His pulse is getting weak. We need to move him." They prep him and start to move.

"What hospital?" Canaan barks out.

"Summerlin." The medic says quickly before they rush out of the room. I feel like my whole world tilts on its axis. My legs give out, and Seb grabs me before I can collapse.

"I'm not going to charge any of you with impeding an investigation. If you wouldn't have found him when you did, he'd probably be dead already." He turns to look at Canaan. "As for you Devlin, don't ever go against a direct order again."

"Sir, I did what any one of us would have done. Be pissed all you want, but I wasn't going to be sitting on my ass while these bastards had Spencer. I don't regret going to them for help." Canaan motions to us and I see the admiration in Prez's face. He likes when you stand up for what you believe in. He may not have liked it when Brant stood up to him for Anslie, but he gets it.

I cradle my wrist to my stomach, I try to stop leaning on Sebastian. I need to get to the hospital to make sure Spencer makes it out alive. He deserves life, not death. He doesn't need the death cloud that is hovering over the Saints to affect his life any more than it has today. Once I know he's okay, I'm setting him free of me. Free of the danger and drama that my life seems to be made up of.

"You should get that looked at," Dixon says eyeing my wrist. "It might be broken." I look down at my wrist and see that it's swelled twice the size of my other one.

"Come on. We can get you showered and to the hospital. We can check on Spencer while were there." I nod my head and watch as the rest of the guys make their way towards the door and out of the building.

Seb and I trail behind them, and before we can make it out of the room, Dixon stops us. "I'm sorry I forced him to break your trust. Thank you for finding him." Words fail me. Instead of responding, I nod my head slightly and start to walk again.

The whole ride back to the clubhouse is a blur. My heart hurts in a way I never thought possible. Seeing the blood pour out of Spencer scarred me in a way I don't think I'll survive. He didn't

deserve that. He deserves the world.

"You good?" Dom asks from his place across from me.

"Yeah." My voice cracks and I know he can see the truth written all over my face. The truth is I'm not okay. I don't know if I ever will be either.

After going through the motions at my place with River tending to me like I'm a child, I'm finally standing buck naked in my shower, watching the river of red run down the drain in front of me. She stripped me down and forced me into the shower once I walked in the house.

"Elijah?" She calls from right outside the shower. I close my eyes and take a deep breath.

"Yeah, babe?" My voice is hoarse, and I know it's from the emotions that are flooding my system.

"Is he going to be okay?" River is an innocent still. She knows the men we can be after we attacked that fucker who sent her the pictures, but she doesn't know everything we will do to ensure that our family is protected.

"I don't know." I rest my forehead against the shower wall, and I can hear the hitch in her voice when she responds again.

"I hope he's okay. He's changed you, and I don't want you to lose the best thing you've had because of your job differences. I love you Elijah, and I just want you to be happy."

I can't force any more words out of my mouth. She's right, but I'm not going to say anything. Having his blood on my hands made me realize I need to let him go. For the first time ever, I'm going to not be selfish. I won't keep him all to myself; I'm letting him be free. Free of the life I live and the conflict of interest with his job.

Washing the rest of the blood off me, I wash my hair quickly and shut the water off with my good hand. Reaching out of the shower, I grab a towel and wrap it around my waist. Stepping out, I see River sitting on the toilet seat. A frown is permanently on her face right now. She stands up and moves towards me, wrapping her arms around my waist and pressing her cheek to my chest.

"I already know what you're going to do." Her voice is soft and sad. I close my eyes and rest my cheek on the top of her head. "Just know that I'll always be on your side."

"Thank you, babe." I murmur.

"Now let's get you dressed so you can get that checked out," she looks up at me and forces a fake smile on her lips.

EPILOGUE

Spencer

Six Months Later

Walking into the bar, I am finally starting to feel like myself again. I haven't heard from Elijah since the night I was kidnapped. Although part of me hates him for not coming to see me in the hospital, I get it. I talked to Canaan when I woke up, and he told me that Elijah was the one who saved me. Elijah was the one who stopped some of the bleeding as I laid on the ground of that shitty warehouse.

The first place I head is to the bar. Part of me doesn't even know why I'm here right now, but the other part has been craving a glimpse of the man I fell in love with. It's been six months since the kidnapping and not a day goes by that I don't think about him.

The feel of his rough hands as they slid over my skin, the sweet kisses he placed on my neck, and the rough sex he made me crave.

After the bartender drops my drink off, I grab it and take a long pull. The alcohol burns as it goes down, but it reminds me that I'm still living.

I didn't expect to live through that night. To be honest, without him by myself this whole time I would have rather that bullet kill me. I lost a lot that night. I lost the trust of the man I'm so fucking stupidly in love with, got put on restrictive duty at work, and that I was the reason he had to come out before he was ready.

Walking through the crowded bar, I scan the faces and stop on a familiar one. Walking towards her, I see the forced smile on her face. She's beautiful in the girl next door sort of way that drives straight men nuts. "Hey River." I greet when I come to a stop in front of her. Her eyes scan me over, and I just hope she will mention seeing me tonight to Elijah.

"Hey, Hun!" She smiles fakely while leaning in to kiss my cheeks. "I didn't expect to see you here tonight." She murmurs in my ear. Her arms wrap around me, and she pulls me into a hug.

"Yeah, I've been on restricted duty. I don't get to do all the fun stuff while I'm still recovering from the broken femur." She frowns and then her eyes start to track something behind me. When I turn to see what she's looking at, I don't see anything.

"So what are you doing here?" I ask. It's none of my business, but if she's here, he can't be too far away.

"I was actually hoping that I'd run into you." She is now messing with her hands and won't look me in the eyes.

"What can I do for you?" I'm now curious. Maybe she is here by herself.

"First, I want to say how sorry I am that I only visited you once. I feel like such a terrible person. I just knew how hard it was on Elijah when he found out I went to see you." I nod my head in understanding. If Canaan said he went to see Elijah, I'd be pissed and hurt. I have no idea why, but it would sting.

186

"Don't be sorry. It isn't your fault. I was the one who broke his trust. I didn't expect him to stick around." I run my hand over my few days old beard.

"He's been miserable," she says quietly.

"He's not the only one." I laugh dryly.

Her frown gets worse, but she doesn't say anything else. I wrap an arm around her and pull her into me. "I'm glad I got to see you." She rests her head on my shoulder, and I feel a vibration come from her. She grabs her phone from her pocket and glances at the screen. A small grin forms on her lips and she looks up at me.

I give her a strange look, but her grin only gets bigger. She shows me the screen, and I see Elijah's name.

Elijah: **Why don't you find a man of your own?**

I feel my brows scrunch together in confusion before a hand lands on my shoulder. Turning around, I see Elijah's face staring right at me.

Staring into his eyes, I feel like I can finally breathe again. The dark cloud feels like it's finally lifting. "Spence." His voice is rough, and I can see the bags under his eyes. Reaching out, I run my hand along his cheek, and he leans into my touch. "Fuck I've missed you."

Instead of saying something back to him, I end up punching him in the gut. He wasn't expecting it by the 'oomph' he lets out.

"I know I deserve that." His voice is lower, and it turns me on even though I'm pissed. I wasn't sure how I was going to react when I saw him again, but I never thought I'd hit him in the gut.

"You deserve more than that," I grunt out. My hands are shaking and as mad at him as I am; I still can't fight the pull he has over me.

He wraps an arm around my neck and pulls me into his body. His arms wrap around me, and he doesn't let me go. "I fucked up. I know I did, but I'm tired of living without you." His nose gently touches mine and I know I'm done for. He slightly bites his lip as he waits for me to say something. "I shouldn't have left you that night. I should have come to the hospital to sit by your side. I was a coward." His gray eyes darken, and I see the anger and hurt in them.

"My pride was bruised, I was scared that I had lost you, and my family just found out I was gay. I know it's not an excuse, but I'll prove to you every damn day that I'm in it with you. Now and forever." His mouth comes closer to mine, and the only thing I can think about is feeling his lips on mine again. Instead of saying anything, I crush my mouth against his and kiss him like he's the oxygen that I need.

I hear River's catcall from next to us, and I can't help but grin against his lips. It feels like coming home.

"Spence," Elijah growls. I roll over and come face to face with him. His eyes are light gray right now, and I can feel his hardness from here. After we had reconnected at my place, he dragged me back to Las Vegas where I got to meet his family.

Let's just say that meeting them was an awkward, but enjoyable experience. His mom was a delight and his sister-in-law Anslie was to die for. She is tiny, but can pack a mean punch if you fuck with her.

His brothers didn't really seem all that put out by me, but his father still had a scowl on his face. "What?" I finally ask him.

He's running his hands down my back, and I can't help but curl my body into his further.

"Thank you." His eyes scan over my face. I reach up and cup his cheek. I don't know why he's thanking me. I didn't do anything that I normally wouldn't do. All I've done is love a man that is so different than me. We are opposites in every way, but stand for the same things in a way.

He'd do anything to protect the family he was born into and the family he joined. I would do the same. The Saints have opened my eyes to a lot of things that I would never have believed if I didn't see it firsthand. They aren't the bad guys that the files at the office said. They are family oriented and would do anything to protect their own. Who wouldn't?

"You don't have to thank me. I'm just glad I was the one you picked out of a bar full of men. You've taught me a lot, but most of all you've taught me what love really is." I run my hand through his hair, and he kisses my lips.

"I love you, Spence," he mumbles against my lips.

"I love you too, my sexy biker." He grins at the nickname, and I can't help but feel right where I belong.

THE END

A Sneak Peek at:

Wayward Deviance

The Wayward Saints, MC

Book Eight

K. Renee

K. RENEE

CHAPTER ONE

Bentley

I never understood what the fuck my brothers thought when they decided to get shacked up with women. One woman for the rest of your life sounds pretty fucking pathetic. We are the Wayward Saints and got enough ass to last us a lifetime. Once upon a time ago, they all used to think the same way I do. Love them and leave them was the only motto we lived by.

Hell as kids, all of us were chomping at the bit to lose our virginities. I was the youngest, so my brothers would always talk about the pussy they were tapping. They would tell me about sex and all the things they did to girls. My interest was always peaked, but when I finally lost my virginity at fifteen, I didn't get what they were talking about. I didn't have the same orgasms that they talked about. Hell, I had a hard time just getting off with the girls from high school.

At seventeen, I finally figured out what they were talking about. My first full blown orgasm was with a club whore who liked things a little rougher than the rest. Hell, I had no idea what she wanted, but she walked me through it every step of the way. And fucking hell was it phenomenal.

The moment my palm landed on her pale white ass, I knew that I finally found something that I liked. Judging by the moans that came out of her mouth, I was doing something right. Seeing my hand print on her ass got me harder than I had ever been before. She reached behind and squeezed my balls, and I almost fucking came right then and there.

I didn't know why I was programmed this way, but Silvie always made sure to get me off when I needed it. We used each other, and we were both okay with it. I was afraid of how my brothers would react if I told them that I just couldn't get it up for any of the bitches who wanted to fuck missionary only. It wasn't my taste and I sure as hell didn't want just to get them off.

Being the youngest boy in my family, I was selfish. My old man always gave me what I wanted because he felt bad that I didn't get to spend as much time as my brothers did with my mom.

He blamed himself for her death, and I did too for a long time.

When I turned eighteen and started prospecting, I realized that there was nothing he could have done. That same thing could happen to any of the members, and we were lucky to have her in our lives for the short amount of time that we did.

For the last few years, I've been watching my idiot brother's fall in love. My sister, yeah she's a different story. I always hoped that she would find a man who could take care of her and still be able to deal with us. And trust me when I say my brothers and I can be a handful.

We used to love to screw with the little high school boys she tried to date. Not one of them came to the house without pissing themselves. Robbie and I made it a mission to scare them off before they could even get to the front door, something that Anslie would frown at.

When I found out about her and Brant, I wanted to put my fist through his face. He sure as hell didn't deserve her, no man did. She was our baby sister, and we would do anything to protect her, even if that meant we went against one of our own.

Before Brant was sent to Oregon, I could see that something was going on between them, hell all of us could. It wasn't ideal, but he made her happy and protected her when we weren't around. I was okay with that. Plus, I could see that she really dug him. I was glad he finally pulled his head out of his ass and finally manned up. At first, I thought I would have to beat his ass for the way he leads her on. She had his twin sons, but he was still attached to that bitch he was with when Ans came back.

My brothers and I talked about beating his ass on more than one occasion just because he knocked her up and never once told us about it. I went after him one night, and Robbie had to hold me back.

Sure I'm the youngest of the Davoli boys, but I can fuck your shit up just like my older brothers. Who do you think taught me?

The minute Brynn walked into my life; I knew I was in for a hell of a ride. That girl was hell in heels, and I couldn't keep my eyes off of her. Her tight little black shorts and skimpy tops left nothing to the imagination, and I couldn't wait to sink balls deep into her. Her white blonde hair spilled down her back in waves, and the only thing I could think of was wrapping it around my arm and bending her over the first thing I could find.

The one catch was that she didn't know about the thoughts that were constantly running through my head. She's a good girl with a wild streak a mile long, but I'm sure this was still a little too much for her tastes.

Sure the sexy little thing made it difficult to concentrate at work, but I wouldn't give up my lifestyle for her. I need the release, and I only know one way of getting it.

Over the years I've ruined more girls than I could count with the things I wanted. I wanted so bad to ruin Brynn, but my sister would fucking kill me. Anslie and Brynn have gotten really close over the last few months. Brynn works in the bike shop as the receptionist or some shit, and for weeks I've been thinking about sinking into her sweet pussy.

Shit, I thought for sure my dick was gonna explode when I walked in on her bent over her desk just now.

Her tight little shorts were showing off just enough of her ass cheeks to turn even gay men straight. She had no panty lines so I can only imagine what she had on underneath. I have to bite the inside of my cheek to keep from reaching over and grabbing her ass.

I clear my throat, and she jumps. Sometimes, I swear she doesn't know how fucking hot she is.

"Bentley." She stutters.

I smirk at her and walk as close as I can without touching her. I watch the way her throat bobs with each swallow she takes, and my hands are itching to be on her neck. She's nervous, and it turns me on even more.

"Hey, darlin'. How are things going?" I ask.

What I would give to be able to bend her over this desk and fuck her into next year.

Brynn doesn't have a lot of curves, but I can bet money that she would look fucking perfect tied to my bed.

Licking her lips, I watch her eyes turn lustful, and I know

she wants me just as bad as I want her.

"They are great." She whispers. "I am finally getting the hang of things around here." I watch her eyes trail down my body, and I get hard. When she gets to my dick, I hear her sharp intake of breath. She can see what she does to me, and I would love to turn her ass pink with my hand.

The office door opens, and I hear my nephews come in screaming, "Unkle Benwee!" I turn around and get slammed into by Severye and Remington. I look up from my favorite mini people and see my sister staring daggers at me. She has Braxton on her hip, and he's pulling on her hair. "Hey, Brynn!" She says with a huge smile.

"Bentley." She says. I walk over to her and grab my favorite little boy out of her arms.

Kissing her on the cheek, I reply. "Hey, little girl."

She sticks her tongue out at me and tells me she's not the youngest anymore. I laugh at her because she will always be a little girl to us. Anslie and I are only three years apart, so I wasn't as overbearing as Dom or Robbie. I let her do as she pleased and only stepped in when necessary.

"Can you watch the boys for me, Ben?" She asks sweetly. Shit. I should have known better.

"Come on little girl. I'm working. Can't you get your old man to watch his kids? I know that bastard ain't here working."

She gives me her signature puppy dog eyes and I pretty much give in. "I want to spend some time with Brantley alone. I'll love you forever Benny."

I hate when she calls me that. "You already love me forever sis. But yeah I watch the little people."

She squeals and wraps her arms around my neck, and Brax grabs her hair again. She kisses my cheek and then pulls her hair out of his grasp. She gives the boys each a kiss and tells them that she loves them.

"Bye guys, love you. Thanks, Ben. Bye Brynn!" She runs out the door, and I turn to look at Brynn who has a smile on her face.

"What?" I ask with a smirk.

She shakes her head, and her white blonde hair danced around her face. "Just didn't expect you to be the type to watch your sister's kids."

Looking over at the twins, they are playing cars on the desk and not even paying attention to what's going on. I walk over to her and lean into her ear. "I'm a lot of bad things darlin', but I love these little guys and would do anything for them and my sister."

I feel her body break out into goose bumps and Brax tries to grab her hair. I angle him away just enough so he can't grab the stands.

"You can't be all that bad if you babysit for your sister." She states unevenly. I'm affecting her, and I can't help but smile.

"Trust me; I'm all sorts of fucked up." I lean away from her and look into her eyes. She looks fascinated, but I can tell she still isn't sure about me.

Every ounce of me wants to dominate her, but in the back of my mind, I know that I can't ruin her. She's too good for the likes of me. And I'll be damned if I hurt her when every instinct in me wants to protect her.

She reaches out and places her hand on my arm. "Bentley,

you can't be that bad."

Brax starts to babble about who knows what, but I can only focus on the blonde beauty standing in front of me.

"You have no idea," I state staring into her icy blue eyes. I hear the door slam open, but I don't remove my eyes from her.

"Bentley!" The bitch shrieks! Fuck me. I told this cunt to get lost and she still doesn't fucking get it. Slowly turning around I come face to face with the bitch I wish I never let in my bed.

The bitch tries to look around me, but I tower over Brynn, so she's covered from her sights. Shit would get real ugly fast if she knew all the things I've been thinking about Brynn.

Handing my nephew Brax to Brynn, I face the bitch. Yeah, I call her bitch. No, it's not a pet name, and yes it's how I feel about her. She's a bitch plain and simple. She thinks that just because we fucked a few times that we are suddenly in a fucking relationship. Every fucker that knows me knows I don't do relationships. Bitches are only good for one thing.

"What do you want?" I ask clenching my fists. I've never hit a woman, but this bitch has gone way too fucking far.

"Bentley, we're supposed to go out. Don't you remember our date?" She whines.

I can hear Brynn snickering behind me, and it makes me want to paddle her ass so fucking bad.

"We aren't doing shit. I told you we were done and we will never fuck again." I ground out. I only have so much patience before I flip my shit and this bitch is right there.

I feel Brynn's hand on my lower back, and I have to force myself to focus on the bitch in front of me.

"Baby! We are meant to be together!" She wails.

The twins look over at us, and I cringe. They watch us intently, and I sure hope they don't repeat any of this to my sister. She would be pissed.

"Bitch, get the fuck out of my shop and out of my life. I've told you a hundred times. We. Are. Not. Together." Brax starts to cry, and I decide I would rather pull my teeth out then deal with this shit any longer. I don't want to subject my nephews and Brynn to this crazy bitch any longer.

I push the bitch out the door and into the parking lot.

She turns and huffs out in annoyance. She's lucky. I want to strangle the fucking dumb bitch and not in a good way.

"Bentley." I hold my hand up stopping her from saying anything else.

"No. I fucking told you once that we are done. Don't even come near me again." I watch her eyes get huge, and I can tell she's finally listening to me.

"You pull that shit again, and you will wish you never met me. I'm not fucking around." Before she can say a thing, I turn and walk back to the office and slam the door shut before she can follow me. Not that I think she is that fucking stupid. But hey, I can be wrong.

ABOUT THE AUTHOR

K. Renee is from sunny California. Creative by nature, she decided to put her imagination on paper. During the day, she works in an office; at night, she writes. These stories have been in her head for years and are finally coming out on paper.

http://kreneeauthor.net

https://www.facebook.com/kayreneeauthor

k.renee.author@gmail.com

Tsu: KReneeAuthor

Twitter: k_renee_author

https://www.goodreads.com/user/show/36533772-k-renee

K. RENEE

Wayward Secret

ACKNOWLEDGMENTS

First and foremost, I want to thank everyone for buying this book! I never thought I would be releasing *one* book, let alone writing a whole series. I can't wait for everyone to meet my characters and fall in love with them like I have.

I want to thank my beta readers for giving their honest opinion about the book. Trisha, Christa, Roz, Paige, Michelle, and Tiffany... You ladies are awesome! Sorry if I missed anyone! Thank you for taking time out of your schedules to beta read for me. I can't wait for you to read about Raef next!

To my street team, K's Wayward Ladies... Thank you for all you do! You girls are amazing at pimping my book out to the indie world. Thank you for your support and I can't wait to see what the future brings.

To the readers and fans... I thank each and everyone one of you who come to hang out with me during takeovers, participating in my giveaways! I hope you like this and my future books.

-K

Made in the USA
Middletown, DE
03 February 2022